THE COLD ROOM

Carla Martin is fifteen, a bitchy, clever and irreverant schoolgirl. Her father, who seems more of a stranger to her the older she gets, takes her out of school for a few days' holiday in East Berlin. They stay in a filthy and run-down hotel.

Perhaps Carla half expected sinister goings-on to occur, but her own odd dreams, the tapping on her bedroom wall, her father's strange behaviour, are more than she bargained for. Gradually her suspicions of what is going on around her begin to grow, along with questions about the reality of her perceptions. She pulls aside the wardrobe on the wall from which the tapping seems to come, and what she finds beyond has quite unexpected and horrifying consequences, not only for Carla herself, but for the reader.

Jeffrey Caine brilliantly combines the most devastating psychological insight into the mind of a young girl with a thriller-writer's ability to create tension and drama. With this, his second novel, he is likely to establish his reputation as one of our most remarkable young writers.

THE COLD ROOM

Jeffrey Caine

W. H. ALLEN · London
A Howard & Wyndham Company
1976

Printed and bound in Great Britain by Butler & Tanner Ltd, Frome and London for the publishers, W. H. Allen & Co. Ltd, 44 Hill Street, London W1X 8LB

ISBN 0 491 01628 X

To the memory of my grandparents

PART ONE

ONE

The rush, the suddenness of being pulled out of school weeks before the end of term, the last-minute changes, the sweatiness of the travelling—it had all thrown her. She was hot and belligerent. It was only now, in the train to London, that Carla had time to draw back and think about everything, to sort out her mind while her body cooled.

She mopped her face with an Allfresh pad, which came away grime-streaked, and lit a cigarette. Then she sniffed under her arms and pulled a face. Uncool, in both senses. Being rushed destroyed her poise, left her vulnerable—bad because mood was talismanic and because with Hugh she had decided to cut ice with ice.

She found herself outstaring an oldish woman opposite, a biddy in a blue felt hat with a pin through it. The woman looked disapproving; she sniffed eloquently, her eyes dropping to the cigarette in Carla's fingers. Carla stared back, flashed a saccharine smile (wonderful for aggravating hostility) and considered hawking noisily on the floor to get a reaction. But she was distracted by the city type next to her, a man who with six clear inches between himself and the window, insisted on pressing up against Carla, casually spreading himself so that their thighs made contact, then jerking suddenly away as though that wasn't what he'd intended at all. His *Times* lay across his lap, asking to be snatched away. It was a delicious hate she felt towards them both, the gent and the biddy. The gent reminded her slightly of Hugh, and that helped. So let either of them start something. She was just in the mood. Someone pick on her, please. But the puckered lips under the blue felt hat muttered sub-vocally and the pin-striped thigh merely twitched. Carla jerked her leg and her mind away.

Although the panic stage was only a couple of hours old, the other, the feeling of being manipulated, was something she'd lived with for a long time. It confused her, made her defensively prickly. And that

9

suited her well enough, she supposed, because in a world full of probing fingers you needed prickles or a shell or something, to protect your soft places. The thought reminded her of the city type, and she borrowed a moment from her thoughts to half-turn and stare at him. He made an exactly equal and parallel turn, like the other half of a perfectly choreographed dance duo, and stared at a field of sheep. Some of the sheep were lying down. The rest were grazing. Sunny periods with showers. Why did everything always have to be so indeterminate?

Like her state of mind, which ought to have been simply, straightforwardly imbecile-happy at being out of school early and on the way to a place she'd never been before ('Think how exciting, Carla, dear.' She'd thought. It wasn't. But it *should* have been, it bloody should.) with a fascinating tall, dark stranger, a balding, middle-aged, medium-tall, dark stranger who just happened to be her father. That was typical Carla, that. Nothing was simple, her whole *Weltanschauung* like a three-dimensional geometric problem in Chinese. Which probably explained why for six months she'd been on her Anne Frank kick, envying that fantastic, girlish bloody exuberance about everything, everything from the first flowers of spring to the latest tit-bit of war news to the loss of her fountain-pen. It was envy, and jealousy she felt, and tremendous pity-sort-of-compassion—*Mitempfinden*—but most of all it was worship because of the incredible way Anne had *stood* it all those years without going nuts, and not only stood it but relished so much of it. The key was simplicity. Not naivety, but simplicity of soul, which Carla didn't have. One single day in Anne's Secret Annexe would drive her screwy. God, just dreaming about it was enough.

That was last night, loathsome boiled-fish night. She'd dreamed about being in Anne's Secret Annexe, except that the place she'd been in wasn't Anne's Annexe. It was difficult to remember what had been different about her own dream-Annexe because she'd made one of her self-control efforts to remove the dream to a dusty Unwanted section of her mind. Now that she wanted it again she couldn't find it. Great stuff, self-control. But at the time the dream had been lucid enough to give her the screaming willies, only thank Freud the screams were silent ones or she'd have woken the entire dorm. She recollected bits of it, though. The Annexe itself. It had been a one-roomed affair, sort of psychic bedsit, but without a window (she wasn't sure about the window), and she'd been alone in there. No Van Daans, no Margot, no Dussel, not even her father. The weirdest part of the dream, though, was that someone's father had been in it, in the dream but not in the Annexe. He'd been outside, trying to get into the Secret Annexe, a big man who said he was her father, but she didn't recognise in him the genial Otto Frank of the Diary. The father in her Anne Frank dream was someone she had to keep out, because he terrified her. He'd been gross and obscene and had shouted threats at her through the wall.

Before filing the thing away in Unwanted Carla had allowed Marsha a peep at it, and Marsha had made her do their psychoanalysis bit, complete with couch and thick Austrian accent. 'Zis dream reflects your attitude to your fazzer, mein Kind. Vot it means iss zat you are afraid of him, ja? Ze little dark room in vich you vere hiding represents your subconscious mind vile slipping, from vich you were trying to shut out ze unvelcome image of your fazzer, ja? How'm I doing?' 'Unsubtle,' she'd said, and Marsha had taken offence and stopped the game.

But it *was* unsubtle, because the whole thing about Hugh—her real father—was infinitely more complex than that. At least it seemed so to her, on the train that was taking her to meet him. But then maybe she was so used to seeing complexities that she'd taken to seeing them when they weren't even there. And if so, how the hell did you get out of a bind like that? Like trying to see the end of your own nose. You'd go mentally cross-eyed.

In an hour or so she'd be seeing him in the flesh, as they said, the true, thrilling hunk of father making his first personal appearance since last season, and would he please autograph her nightmare? Oh, the dirty thrill of the cohabitation (was that the right word?) ahead of them in Deutschland, sordidity in technicolour and all miraculously Untouched by Human Hand. Now that was the *echt* Hugh Martin, the way he'd engineered everything, the unseen watchmaker, the grand puppetmaster. Not hard to see where her own deviousness came from, was it? Toothy McClean had called her into the famous 'little room' for one of her equally famous tête-à-têtes, and she'd got the full, gushing, smarmy McClean treatment—crows' feet smiles by the yard and all things bright and Teutonic. Then Toothy had unfolded a typewritten letter and before she'd read a word of it, Carla had known it was from Hugh and even roughly what Hugh's message was. Afterwards she'd broken the news to Marsha in their private smoking place beyond the playing fields. They spread their blazers on the damp grass and smoked, Carla, the tragic heroine manipulated by the Fates, leaning back on the carefully frayed elbows of her summer cardigan. Phaedra blowing smoke rings.

'The summer's buggered,' she'd announced. 'We've had Geneva. I've had it, anyway. Geneva's scrapped. Forget it. Someone saw me looking happy and got the word back.'

'What did she say, for God's sake?'

'Berlin.'

'Berlin!'

'East bloody Berlin.

'Jesus.'

'Right.'

'Who with? Toothy?'

'No, you tit. *Him.*'

Then Marsha had said, 'Oh, no,' and she'd said, 'Oh bloody yes,' and the rest was redundant. Eventually Marsha had found a bright side to look on, pointing out that it would get Carla out of end-of-term Social Projects (big deal), and that at least it would give Carla a chance to get to know him better, which earned her a filthy look because He had said that in the letter, that being his absolutely sole raison de ruiner her summer, and who wanted to get to know Him better anyway? In the end they had both fallen into flat misery and skipped afternoon school as a grand gesture of *Weltschmerz*.

'I'm not bloody going,' Carla told the dorm that evening.

'Abscond, Carla,' someone said.

'Commit suicide,' another girl suggested.

Then, the next morning, that screamingly hilarious follow-up letter arrived: Phase Two of Hugh Martin's Grand Design, the

Personal Touch. Hugh was suddenly Fifth Arts property. Marsha read the letter aloud to the dorm, a ruler stuck in her mouth.

' "It seems worthwhile for two reasons," ' Marsha read, puffing hard on the ruler. ' "First, because we have seen so little of each other in the past year that I'm afraid we will become strangers to each other . . ." '

'Too late,' Carla said. 'Happened already.'

'Shut up. "Secondly, because a prolonged stay in Germany, as well as giving us an opportunity to 'catch up' . . ." Why's he put "catch up" in inverted commas?' She shrugged. ' ". . . to 'catch up', will be extremely good for your German." Oh, *extremely*.'

'Extremely, darling.'

'But oh, so terribly truly extremely so, don't you know.'

' "We·shall be arriving in East Berlin on 4 July, probably some time in the late evening; so I would advise you to be sure of getting a good night's sleep in advance." Very sensible man, Carla.' Marsha wagged her finger. ' "Long journeys, as you will know, can be very tiring." God, it's pure Lord Chesterfield.'

'Told you. He thinks I'm eleven. Might turn up in pigtails. What d'you think?'

'Great. Can I do them for you?'

'No thanks. He'd probably make that an excuse for tucking me in at seven o'clock every night.'

'And kissing you night-nights,' Marsha said, pursing her lips. 'I love this bit about packing suitable clothes. What's he trying to say?'

'Fatherese for knickers. What sort of impression do you get of him, Marsh?'

Marsha screwed up her face. 'Sort of weird.'

'That's Hugh.'

'Queer. Not queer queer. Just odd-queer. When did you see him last?'

Carla worked it out. 'Not counting phone calls, last August. For about two days. And that was a big deal because he was between books. Before that, five days the previous Christmas. In London. He's so devoted, you see.'

The girls had been keen to know what Carla's father looked like.

13

'Hugh,' Marsha mused. 'Hughie. I see Hughs as pointy-nosed dumps with thin blond-type hair, falling out, and shabby raincoats. Bit on the seedy side.'

'He's got fishy lips,' Carla said. 'Think I've got his lips?'

'Depends. What sort of fish?'

'Salmon.'

'You're more trouty.'

'Charming.'

The girls had tried to build a composite picture of Hugh Martin, supplying Hughish characteristics for Carla to grade on a ten-point scale.

'Etox accent?'

'More BBC. Seven.'

'Wears three-piece suits and regimental ties.'

'Seven. No, eight. But not regimental. Old School, I think.'

'Leather baccy pouch filled with Balkan Sobranie.'

Carla hesitated over the tobacco. 'It stinks, anyway,' she confirmed. 'The pouch is plastic. Yellow plastic. Five. Next.'

'Reads *The Times* and votes Tory.'

'No marks for that. Anyway, I'm not sure it isn't *The Guardian*. Next.'

'Drives a Jag.'

'Rover. Last year's was. Er, six.'

'Does he shave on Sundays?'

'No idea. Don't think I've ever seen him on a Sunday. Can't remember.'

'Hey,' one of the girls called, looking at the letter. 'He's signed it "Hugh".'

'That's what I call him.'

'Fantastic,' the girl said, impressed.

'What do you call yours, then?'

The girl made a face. 'Daddy.'

'What're his books like, Carla?' someone asked, and Carla, nonchalant, answered: 'Never read one. Boring, I should think.' But she'd read the one on Jerusalem, number four in the Unknown Cities of the World series, and had found it mildly interesting though a bit verbose. *East Berlin* would be number six.

14

And then that last-minute change of plan, Hughier than Hugh. The letter said he would pick her up from school himself on the morning of 4 July, and she'd had the whole Arts Fifth lined up to see him; instead of which a taxi had turned up to collect her, and simultaneously she'd got a pompous telegram (trust Hugh to master pomposity in telegraphese) instructing her to meet him at Heathrow and giving times of connections. The taxi had eight minutes to get her to the station. She'd thought that a brilliantly disruptive move by Hugh, hated it, but admired it as first-rate match play. It threw her into the vulnerable state of confusion from which she was only now beginning to recover. Everything seemed to happen at the same time. She could have held her breath while the driver told her he couldn't do the station in less than seven minutes, while Toothy McClean materialised like ectoplasm out of her 'little room' and tucked a small red book into Carla's hand ('A little dated, I'm afraid, but you may find it useful'), then dematerialised as Carla came out of her trance to find herself already in the taxi, no time for a drawn-out ritualistic parting from Marsha, Marsh crying at her through the taxi window and that setting Carla off on a weeping jag, and then the two of them hugging each other through the car window. All of it in a breath. In the next breath Marsha promising to write three times a day like medicine and to include oodles of subversive political stuff and porn to test the East German censorship, Carla promising to do the same. They had time to use the latest catchphrase through the open window, Marsha shouting: '*So* good for your German, Carla, dear,' and herself answering: 'Yes, Fritz will *adore* Berlin *so*, if only he'd expose himself more to the tongue, and I mean the native tongue, la-la,' which jollied over the parting. Marsha blew her a kiss as the taxi pulled away in a spray of gravel.

Carla smiled. The city type had manœuvred his hot thigh inch for inch alongside hers, and was starting to apply steady pressure. She turned to him.

'I've been told I've got to expose myself,' she said.

The man blanched, jumping up.

'My headmistress said it's very good for me to expose myself. My father agrees.'

15

The man moved to another carriage.

'To the language,' Carla explained sweetly to the biddy in the felt hat. 'To my German. My German must come first, don't you think? In fact, it's considered very polite in Germany for the gentleman to come before the lady. More fun, though, if they come at the same time.'

Hugh met her off the squat airport bus. As he placed his hands on her shoulders and leaned forward slightly to peck her cheek, Carla noted that he was wearing a suede jacket and under it a turtleneck shirt. Four out of ten. This change of image would rate a mention in her first letter to Marsha.

'Good journey?' Carla caught her impulse to answer 'Yes, My Lord,' her imagination dressing Hugh in knee breeches and periwig. But her mood had become offhand by this time, and she found it easy not to laugh. She shrugged instead, ice to cut ice.

He bought her lunch. Then they sat over coffee waiting for their flight to be called. He questioned her about school, exams, the health of cousins she'd stayed with over Easter, and Carla answered with shrugs or monosyllables. She let him make all the running, initiated no conversation, delighted in his embarrassed silences. After a while her father took to reading the menu and playing with his pipe. Once she noticed him scratching at a stain on his jacket, a spot so microscopic it might have been imaginary. They both stood up without a word when their flight was announced.

The Lufthansa jet was all plastic fittings and immaculately laundered antimacassars. Before take-off Carla busied herself with translating airline German, but soon gave up trying to decipher the instructions about lifejackets (they were just as incomprehensible in English) and unfolded her air-sickness bag instead.

Hugh gave her a weak smile, pointing with his unlit pipe. 'Not going to need that, I hope.' Carla put the end of the bag in her mouth and started to blow it up. When it was full of air she scrunched up the end. Hugh was staring at her. Good. She brought up her right hand, open-palmed, closed her eyes, and laughed when she heard him say, 'I trust you aren't thinking of bursting that, Carla.'

16

'Sorry,' she said, handing him the bag. 'Didn't know you wanted to do it.'

Which silenced him nicely.

She pretended to rest, lolling back in her Cleopatra pose against the head cushion, eyes screwed shut. The aircraft began to shriek and vibrate and Carla smacked her lips, needing a nonchalant gesture because she was suddenly fluttering inside. Dear Anne, *timor timendi conturbat me*. The rustle of Hugh's jacket as the smoking sign lit up and he fished for tobacco. Then the statistically dangerous part was over and they were safely floating on cushions of nothing, thousands of feet above ground, impossibly.

'Can't remember if you've flown before,' Hugh was saying.

'Not since I fell out of the nest. My arms get tired.'

She found that with her eyes half open she could watch him unobtrusively, study and learn every gesture, every pose, as ammunition for her letters. He was folding a map, with a *Times* reader's economy of movement, a commuter's unfussed expertise, the pipe clamped between his incisors. That was just another of the thousands of actions she'd never before seen him perform, this stranger who had known her all her life but whom she hardly knew at all. She tried to recall Hugh when her mother had been alive. She remembered that once, at one of the London zoos, he had offered baby Carla to the crocodiles, holding her up at the fence and pinching her chubby arms in demonstration. The crocs weren't buying, he'd said, and tried the tigers. No, not fat enough for them either. Carla remembered the love–hate, thrill–fear of that game, her half—no, quarter—belief that he would feed her, out of whim, to the carnivores, and she had an image of her mother laughing at her tentative disbelief. Hugh hadn't been untouchable in those days. She knew because she could recall the tobacco taste of his mouth, though surprisingly, little else. Only odd unconnected images remained in her memory: the heavy old typewriter stripped of its paint and with the foreign name (Adler?) that he used to sit at, and where occasionally she would perch on his lap and peck at a key. She'd found the keys hard to move and had thought him monstrously strong to make them fly the way he did.

17

Strong but gentle, a benevolent monster, becoming by degrees a nothing, yet always an intimate embarrassment like a wart on the nose. Attached to her somehow, but alien and unwanted. Her father. Something to be covered up.

One day her mother had a lump and went to hospital. Hugh (still 'Daddy' then) had explained to Carla very carefully that the lump was wicked and wanted to eat Mummy from inside. And Carla had wanted to know who had put the lump in there in the first place. Hugh said it had just grown all on its own, but she had never believed that lie. Someone must have put it there. He had offered her to the tigers, so why not feed Mummy to the lump? Then her mother had died and was buried with the lump still inside her (Carla made a point of asking about that), the evidence buried with her. She'd gone away to school and had been a celebrity with a freshly dead mother. She told her new friends about the lump, and about how she suspected Hugh of planting it inside her mother's body. One term she formed a detective society to prove the murder, but since it involved digging up the body (for fingerprints) the society lost impetus.

She glanced at her father; he was exonerated now that she knew the truth about that lump. Why, then, did she still distrust him? He'd folded the map away and was studying a small red book with *Berlin* stamped across the cover in gold leaf. It reminded Carla of the little book Toothy McClean had thrust into her hand a few hours earlier. What had she done with it? She poked through her shoulder-bag and found the book in there, pulled it out and looked at it.

It was a shade thicker than Hugh's book and a darker red, but otherwise its twin. Except that hers was Baedeker's *Germany* and had marbled page ends. He looked up as she opened the book, and she expected him to say 'Snap!' but instead he held out his hand. He gave the Baedeker a glance, then snorted, flipping it closed before he handed it back.

'Where did you pick up that antique?'

'I collect antiques,' she said. 'Didn't know you were valuable, did you?'

'Well don't try and find your way around Berlin with that, Carla. You can use mine.'

'I'll manage.' She tried to look absorbed in the book, but it wasn't until he'd turned back to his own Baedeker that she could concentrate. She smarted from the put-down, felt off-balance in a way she couldn't account for. It was all those quick changes of mood that did it. They made her feel unsure of herself, made her overreact. And the razor edge of her reactions cut her, the wielder, to the bone each time. There seemed to be no way she could strike out without hurting herself in the process. Toothy had said it in her term report, had no right to say it but had said it nonetheless. "Carla's perpetual defensive stance repels friend and enemy alike. Unless she can learn to trust the world a little more and open herself to others, she will ultimately alienate those who love her and have no choice but to turn her violence inwards, upon herself, with possibly disastrous consequences." Cheeky bitch. As if imprinted there by her thoughts, the name appeared on the page. Leipzig: Karl Baedeker, Publisher, 1936, she read. And below it, in faded purple ink, *E. M. McClean, 1938.*

They changed planes at Frankfurt. A BEA Trident took them on to Tempelhof, a noisy, hard-used plane with trembling wing-tips and shuddering innards. They brushed the rooftops of Berlin, it seemed, coming in to land, and for a moment she was certain they would crash. Her thought then was: Ah, so what? That was her mood.

But, despite herself, she brightened after the landing. It was the excitement of the unfamiliar that did it, the shock to her faculties of coming off linguistic auto-pilot; speaking, normally as unconscious a process as breathing, would from now on require the full attention of her mind. It was going to be a lonely experience, like being the only sane one in a mental asylum. It would sharpen the outline of the ego, draw out the adrenalin. She felt alive all at once, as if she had just awoken, yet at the same time embarrassed at the need to thicken her speech and utter German sounds. So she let Hugh talk her through customs and into a Mercedes taxi. The fluency of Hugh's German impressed her. He gave the driver rapid instructions and within minutes (Tempelhof is close to the centre of West Berlin) they were dodging end-of-day traffic in the Kurfürstendamm.

'We'll pick up the hire car,' Hugh told Carla, 'and have something to eat in West Berlin before crossing over. All right with you?'

She nodded distractedly. The city had her attention. Bright, brash, garish, it was a night city, and she sensed this as its nocturnal life can be sensed in the half-closed daytime eyes of a sleepy cat. She wanted to stay there and do nighttime things: walk the wide and crowded boulevards, drink coffee at a pavement table, study the illuminated promises in the windows of chic, expensive shops. The signs said Coca-Cola, as in Piccadilly, and that was right here, appropriate because this was a money place, money the religion locally, and it seemed right to respect it.

'Disappointed?' Hugh was saying. 'It isn't what you expected, is it?'

'Fantastic.' It was nothing like what she'd expected. She tried to call to mind the Berlin of her imagination, to superimpose it on the actual one, the dazzling, light-filled city beyond the taxi window, but the grey phantasm was gone suddenly. All she remembered of it was the wilting iron lampposts and the street signs in heavy Gothic lettering, the soot-fouled stonework of the buildings, and the jack-booted stormtroopers making the pavements ring. Impressions she'd culled from old photographs; photographs that had never been anything but old, old on the day they were taken, like an infant wizened from the womb; like the photographs of Anne and of her Secret Annexe, moments of the past glimpsed through a keyhole in time and never here-and-now, seen in the monochrome shading of yesterday. That world was gone. She realised it almost with disappointment. It was like revisiting a place known from childhood, an old quarter of a great city that had since been rebuilt, and not quite recognising it.

'Fantastic,' she said again. 'Can we stay overnight?'

Hugh became defensive, explained that their hotel rooms in East Berlin were booked from the fourth. The Deutsches Demokratisches Republik was touchy, almost obsessive about such things and might revoke his permit if he turned up a day late. Carla shrugged, to let him know that he had failed her personally in the one concession she'd asked, and that she wasn't about to let her guard slip again in a hurry.

She made do with window shopping while Hugh collected the arc

20

and they ate garlicked pork fillet with spinach at one of the pavement tables on Kurfürstendamm.

'Look,' Hugh said, breaking a twenty-minute silence, 'we can probably manage a few days here on the way back.'

'Big deal.'

Just before nine o'clock they crossed into East Berlin in the red Volkswagen 1300 Hugh had hired from SU Interrent.

They waited in a line of cars for the search and documentation check. With the engine switched off the only sound was the creak of upholstery as Carla shifted position and the drumming of Hugh's fingers on the steering wheel. A kind of tension began to build in her as she sat waiting, nursing a slight heat headache, the sort aspirin wouldn't touch—even if she had any. Lord Chesterfield had been right after all: she was tired, and it had been a long day. But the tension had another source too. It had to do with the crossing, with the Wall and what lay beyond the Wall, with the grey-green uniforms and jackboots of the border guards and the machine pistols they carried. She hadn't felt this in West Berlin, but there was something here that set up vibrations in her windpipe, a sternness, a hardness, a sense that she was entering the lair of some mythical grotesque, a purblind Cyclopean brute that couldn't survive at higher temperatures but lumbered from end to end of its chill confines. Hugh had told her what to expect of the Berlin Wall. 'Don't look for a forty-foot wall,' he'd said, 'like something around Brixton Prison. It extends in depth, not height.' She could see that now in the concrete crash barriers and barbed wire traps of Checkpoint Charlie, where a section had been cut with surgical precision through Berlin. It seemed morbid of them to do that to the city, wanton, like chopping a worm in half with a spade just to see if it was true what they said about worms. It frightened her.

'Impressed?' Hugh said. 'You're along the seam of the world here. One day the whole fabric of civilisation could rip right along it, where we're sitting at this moment.'

'Did you think that up yourself? That metaphor about seams and things?'

'I believe so.'

21

'Thought so. Sounded home-made.'

'What's wrong with it?'

'Bit melo,' she said, and yawned.

'Mellow?'

'Melodramatic.'

'Oh. Well it's a melodramatic place, Carla.'

A man in a business suit got out of the car in front of them and began pulling papers from an inside pocket one at a time, with the air of a conjurer producing scarves from a sleeve.

'In a minute or two,' Hugh said heavily, 'they'll want to search the car. We'll have to get out. Don't worry about it. It's the usual procedure.'

'Who's worried?'

'And please don't be sarcastic to them, Carla.'

'Me? Sarcastic?'

'East–West frontier guards have absolutely no sense of humour. If anything, they have a minus sense of humour. Less even than me.'

'Less than you, Hugh?'

'I thought that would please you.'

A border guard pulled open the car door and waved them out. They waited in an inspection hut while the car was checked. Meanwhile, a pot-bellied guard with a cold sore under his nose scrutinised their visas. For some reason she found it comforting that the man had a bad cold. The puffy upper lip made him less forbidding, reduced him to a comical figure and so robbed him of the power to inspire fear. One of her favourite childhood stories had featured an ogre with a streaming cold. She'd loved that ogre with his laughable threat to eat children for his 'didder'.

'The Great Dictator,' she stage-whispered to Hugh.

'Cut it out, Carla.'

'Film Society had it last term,' she said, as if in explanation, watching the avuncular guard lift Hugh's portable typewriter to head height so that he could examine its underside. 'What's he looking for?'

Hugh didn't answer. His pipe, unlighted, dangled from his mouth.

The guard with the cold pushed Hugh's stuff roughly aside and began on Carla's vanity case. As he went through its contents, turning over nightdresses and underclothes, she had the ridiculous feeling that he would find something incriminating, that he'd find what she was hiding even though she was hiding nothing. The guilt feeling made her flippant. 'Perv,' she said as he pushed the case back to her with its lid still open. The guard clicked his fingers, gesturing for the shoulder bag. 'Rude beast.' He pulled everything out of the bag, then stuffed it all back except the two books. He smiled at the Baedeker and muttered a comment. 'What'd he say?' she asked Hugh.

'Same thing that I said. The Germany that guide book describes doesn't exist any more. He recommends a visit to the Museum für Deutsche Geschichte. I agreed with him.'

The guard was looking through her paperback edition of Anne Frank's Diary, obviously puzzled by it, unsure how to classify it. 'It's just a book,' Carla said. 'Es ist nur ein Buch, ein Tagebuch.'

The man nodded, flicked the cover with his fingernail. When he spoke it was to Hugh, not to her. She caught the word *Buch*, and there was something about the DDR, and Deutschland, and, sticking out like a broken bone, *Nazismus*. It gave her a small shock to hear that word. She tried to catch the man's eye, but he'd already pushed her things to one side and was emptying someone else's bag on to the splintery wooden surface.

'He said he's glad you've come to the DDR, Carla. Judging from your mobile library he thinks you've got the wrong impression of Germany. He wants you to see for yourself that all traces of Nazism have been eradicated. I'd say he has a point. We complain that they have a Dickensian impression of London. They've a right to expect us not to see Isherwood's Berlin, which hasn't existed for thirty years.'

The guard was looking her way again. Carla smiled sweetly. 'Hope your cold turns into pneumonia,' she called, and had the satisfaction of seeing the man nod.

After the noise and brightness of West Berlin it was the quietness that struck her first, and the bad lighting—as if somebody pennypinching on high was cutting down on the electricity bills. Half-way along Friedrichstrasse they crossed Unter den Linden—busier, but still with a suburban feel—then swung right, skirting the Wall, through

23

Prenzlauerberg. The drab sameness of it all made Carla want to weep. Once or twice the car followed a broad avenue and she saw high, modern concrete-and-glass structures, once an all-steel sculpture, but most of their route was through dim streets, many of them cobbled. It was unbelievable after West Berlin, this place that looked like a vast archaeological find, a complete city recovered intact, like Pompeii, from a catastrophe of the past. The few people she saw might have been the excavators, photographed for the newsreel in monochrome; animated, three-dimensional photographs from books about the War, ghosts who didn't know that man had got to the moon or that Everest could be climbed. She saw trams, and the car crossed tram-lines often. Many of the buildings they passed were shabby, shell-pocked antiques with washing strung between them. There were baroque mansions next to bombed sites, overlooking expanses of rubble with half walls standing, some still papered on one side, one with a carved staircase against it leading nowhere. Isherwood's Berlin, whoever Isherwood was. Hitler's capital. Old Berlin. She sensed it.

'What do you think of it?' Hugh asked her at one point.

'Is today a Bank Holiday or something? Like Lenin's wedding anniversary?'

'No, this is fairly typical.'

'It's pathetic,' Carla said. 'Who's Isherwood?'

'Writer. Wrote about Berlin, pre-war Berlin.'

'Would he recognise this place?'

'Ah, I see what you mean. Architecturally it hasn't changed much on this side. The biggest changes are the invisible ones.'

They pulled up eventually outside a sandy-coloured four-storey building in one of the narrower cobbled streets. Its facade had been touched up in one or two places, though mostly it was a leprosy of flaking patches where the rendering had peeled away to reveal old brickwork. There were also a few bullet scars high up near the roof, and around some of the windows.

'This is it,' Hugh said.

'This is what?'

'Granted, it's not very prepossessing. It's probably posher inside.'

24

'This is the hotel!'

'Well, not purpose-built. I'd say a converted tenement.'

'Let's come back when they've finished converting it.'

They crossed the street to the entrance, on one side of which was what looked like a derelict shop. Corrugated iron sheeting had been nailed over its frontage under a faded sign, barely visible. *R. Bruckner: Fleischer* in flaking black paint.

Carla glanced up. They'd even boarded over one of the hotel's windows.

It wasn't posher inside; it was dowdy and depressing and smelled, as she'd guessed it would, of cabbage and decay. Carla's stomach reacted to it. The ache began with the green-painted lobby with its faded, ill-fitting carpet that looked borrowed from somewhere else, and seemed to grow systematically after that, as if it was digesting every detail of the decor: that claustrophobic stairwell (with rounded stone steps, *echt* Early German Peasant), and then the first floor hallway, done in Institution Brown and Sour Cream gloss. And where the paint had peeled, older, dowdier versions of the same colours underneath, as though the walls had been programmed for these shades and no others by some long-dead architect of Bismarck's time.

But what really threw Carla was the dirt everywhere. Every ornate moulding was thick with it, a trap for it; thick grease covered the horizontal surfaces, spotted the papered walls. The concierge— *Inhaberin*, Hugh corrected—was responsible for the state of the place, and the dirt began with her. She led them upstairs to their rooms, a sour-faced old woman reeking of sweat and cabbage water under an outsize pinafore dress in flowered cotton. They followed in her smelly wake as she grunted up the stone steps, Carla wrinkling her nose to Hugh, who carefully avoided looking anywhere but at his feet. She threw open the doors of 116 and 117, adjoining bedrooms with a connecting door, and Carla saw two small rooms that were almost mirror images of each other. Except that something about Carla's furniture was indefinably less austere, a touch more feminine. If she'd been given 116 and no materials, 117 was what she'd have made of it.

She would have used the bedspread for drapes. Hugh's curtains were brown and heavy. Both rooms, though, smelled of mildew and showed damp patches on the wallpaper.

Hugh was grinning. 'Unpretentious, isn't it?'

'God, I feel I want to plunge into a bath every time I touch something, only the bathroom terrifies me more than the dirt.'

'It's last on the left down the hall if you want it.'

'Great. The loo's probably a tin bucket you have to take in turns to empty. Very democratic and all that.'

Hugh laughed. 'I'd be careful, Carla. Frau Holzbaum may speak some English.'

Carla turned suddenly and found Frau Holzbaum scrutinising her. There was something disquieting in the old woman's gaze, an unabashed single-mindedness such as she might have applied to buying meat; Carla seemed to strike her as tender but insubstantial, overpriced but possibly worth buying for all that. Carla stared back, her stomach beginning to swirl. Today was old biddy flag day, all right. Across the continent.

'What do you think of the view?' Hugh was saying.

Without removing her gaze from Frau Holzbaum Carla said, 'Love it. Bricks and other windows with other people behind them looking out on me looking back at them.'

Frau Holzbaum snorted and shuffled out of the room.

'Ah, but this is the real DDR, Carla. Not like those show hotels in Unter den Linden, specially designed for the tourist. That's all fake.'

'I love fake. That old cow was dissecting me with her eyes.'

'I told you, this place isn't on the tourist map. She probably doesn't see many westerners.'

'I don't like her,' Carla said.

'You don't know anything about her, Carla.'

'I don't like her. She smells.' A clinking sound made her turn. Frau Holzbaum was back. She stood in the doorway, fiddling impatiently with her keys, and again her gaze was fixed on Carla. Oh God, Carla thought, the old bitch fancies me. Yuch! She found herself thinking of the witch in Hansel and Gretel. Maybe the old crone was sizing her up for the oven at that. It was an absurd image, a child's fancy, and she should have used it to devastate Frau Holzbaum. But instead it recoiled into her stomach, forcing the garlicked pork upwards, and she had to race for the bathroom with her hand held over her mouth.

TWO

Although her stomach settled quickly it took Carla a long time to fall asleep. It always did in an unfamiliar room, especially a dark one. And even with the curtains open this room was too dark for her. Dark air had greater density, filled a room like black cotton wool. She'd always been afraid to let herself go to sleep under the closely packed black wool in case it smothered her without waking her up. It had been that way for her since she was a small child, though she had never feared the horrors other children feared, never the things that could hide in darkness as much as the tangible darkness itself. She'd remembered to pack her night-light, though, and lay awake by its glow, listening to Hugh moving about next door. When Hugh had gone to bed she concentrated on picking out other sounds, locating them, identifying them, classifying them: thumps, squeaks, clacks, scrapes and taps; pipes knocking together, doors closing on other floors of the building, a car passing in the distance. For a while she played the Helen Keller game, an old comforter for dark nights. She had to close her eyes and cover her head with the cushion for the Helen Keller role, and when the panic began to take over it was time to clasp her right hand with her left and assume the teacher-role, squeezing her hand, then placing it against the teacher's lips and mouthing the words of comfort with her own hot breath, louder and louder until the great breakthrough of that First Whisper . . . Once, years ago, she had wet the bed with excitement while playing the Helen Keller game.

But before long she went back to the noises of the hotel. This time she was Anne Frank in her small bedroom in the Secret Annexe, identifying every sound from the offices below, waiting out the hours till the office closed and she'd be free to move about again, and Margot would be free to cough. For this game it was essential to keep totally still, to relax every muscle in her body but to keep her mind responsive and alert for the dangerous sounds, the unexpected tread on the

28

stair, a car pulling up outside—anything out of the ordinary, anything that might give her a few moments to prepare herself. After a while she became conscious of pain in both her hands, and knew that must be where her nails were cutting into her palms. Rigid with the strain she clenched her fists even harder, wishing it would hurt more so that she might suffer that much more without crying out. When she opened her fists again she found that her hands had gone numb and that the fingers trembled uncontrollably. She released a small sigh, then flopped back on the pillow, drained, disgusted. She understood the disgust. It was for the pretence; not for the self-abuse but because the self-abuse was so pointless and sad, a shoddy thing, a joyless game, a play that never got beyond rehearsal. After the game she would remain smaller than life, unchanged, insignificant. She switched off the night-light and let herself be tortured now by the stifling darkness, knowing that it wasn't enough. Nothing lay in that darkness to threaten her, nor ever would. Inside her, lodged in her like undigested food, was the certain knowledge that this was to be the pattern of her entire life, a meaningless life unbearably long and bland as situation comedy. She imagined Anne Frank surviving, imagined her a smiling fat Hausfrau and mother in her middle forties, anonymous in a suburban garden of Amsterdam, a nothing. She held that image for a while against the pull of sleep, embellished it until it included the husband, Peter Van Daan, now a jowly businessman, and the inevitable brood of colourless nothing children, all teaing vapidly on the lawn on a summer Sunday afternoon. And she found herself there too, in the nauseating tableau: child of the Secret Annexe, Carla Martin, Carla Frank-Van Daan, Christa Bruckner . . .

Somewhere the waking image merged into dream and she was back in the Annexe, all alone in the dark, screaming at some mercifully invisible horror. But she knew, even as she watched the dream pictures flick across her mind, that she'd been unwise to relax her vigilance. A stranger had slipped in unnoticed and it was going to be hard to get her out again. She didn't even know Christa Bruckner.

Hugh knocked on the connecting door at half past eight, then called through the door twenty minutes later, while Carla was pulling on paint-stained jeans and sandals. If Hugh objected to the way she was dressed Carla planned to make the dirt in the hotel her excuse; if he wanted to make an issue of it then that was all right too, and she'd be able to start her campaign against him with make-up, cigarette smoking and Independence—an umbrella term for whatever they might clash over. Vigorously she brushed her long straw-coloured hair, dropped the brush, and when she stooped to retrieve it noticed the droppings for the first time. Before she realised what it was she'd touched one, and had to rush to the bathroom holding her contaminated hand in front of her like a wound, to scour her fingers. Her body vibrating with disgust, she returned to her room and poked at one of the sausage-shaped black pellets with a matchstick. The thing was soft, therefore quite fresh—she shuddered—and big enough to have come from a rat. Her mouth went dry at the thought of rats in her bedroom. That did it. Dirt was one thing, rats were another. She bent down nervously to look along the skirting board. The droppings were scattered every couple of inches along the wall, which was opposite the partition wall with Hugh's room. The trail stopped at a heavy wardrobe, taller than herself, that looked welded into the floor with age. She had a moment's security when she realised that the wardrobe was rat-proof; but all that meant was that no rat could shift it (without help). There was nothing to stop them gnawing through it. Couldn't rats gnaw through mild steel? No, she decided, what she had in her room was a family of friendly, cute little mice with tummy upsets. And anyway she wasn't going to open the wardrobe (her clothes could live on a chair). Hugh could investigate the things, or Frau Biddy. Come up and see my droppings some time. With luck Hugh would turn out to have a horror of vermin, as she knew some men did, and insist on moving to some fantastic hygienic show hotel. Fat chance.

She went down to breakfast.

Hugh and the girl sitting next to him were the only people in the dining room, though at least two other tables showed evidence of breakfasters. The girl, tall, twentyish, with modellish good looks and a slightly too tight blouse, was introduced as Lili something (Schwemmer?).

30

'Lili's our guide,' Hugh added, looking hard at Carla's jeans. The girl looked at them too, then pointedly down at the Jesus sandals. Carla declared war, justifying the loathing she felt for Lili as a gut reaction it would have been immature to ignore. Besides, she was wearing frump's shoes and socks (socks!), and had a broken nail, and the yellow shoulder bag now slung over her chair didn't match the jacket that was also slung over it.

'I was a Girl Guide for a bit,' Carla said, sitting down. 'Chucked it after two weeks. Bit juvenile, don't you think? And that room's disgusting. Yuch!'

'Carla,' Lili said, testing the sound, her ear cocked for the internal echo. 'She could be German.'

Hugh laughed. 'Wait till you hear her accent.'

'No speakee velly good ze Germans. This hotel's got rats.'

'Yes, I understand,' said Lili, pulling a sheet of closely-typed paper from the yellow bag. 'I have your journey plan for the week.' She smoothed the paper. 'Also I have my own car. You car will not be necessary.'

'Rats.'

'Today,' Lili went on, 'General Tour of Berlin and the Museum für Deutsche Geschichte.' She looked at Carla. 'The German History Museum.'

'Oh, I see. "Museum" must mean "museum".'

Lili said, 'How clever she is for thirteen,' which made Hugh laugh.

'Fifteen actually,' Carla said.

'Really?' And to Hugh: 'It will give you historical background to the DDR. Er, perspective. A good foundation to your book.'

Hugh nodded, tapping dottle from his pipe. He sucked its stem.

'Do you smoke, Lili?' Carla said, wondering what Hugh's reaction would be if she lit up. Maybe the bitch smoked and would offer her one.

Lili said, 'If I wanted to kill myself I would choose a quicker way.'

And Hugh had the gall to say 'Quite,' even as he stuffed flake into his Dunhill. Carla glared at them both, hatred churning in her.

They talked about the week's visits without including Carla in the conversation. She tried to draw attention to herself by chewing her

31

nails noisily, then by yawning. She apologised exaggeratedly, in English and in German, at every yawn, until finally Hugh and Lili stopped to look at her.

'Are you still tired, Carla?'

'So sorry. Ich bitte um Verzeihung. Awfully, awfully.'

'Are you trying to tell us something?'

'Perhaps,' Lili suggested, 'she is trying to say she doesn't want to go with us.'

'Are you?' Hugh demanded.

'Isn't this fun? Lili's turn now. Can you guess what I want to say, Lili?'

Lili turned to Hugh. 'Is this an English children's game?'

'I-spy-with-my-little-eye . . . something beginning with B,' Carla said. She chewed on a finger.

'Worüber spricht sie?'

'Nichts,' Hugh said quickly. 'Ein Kinderspiel.'

Lili said: 'Ah, I understand.'

'She understands,' Carla mocked.

'Enough, Carla. Just stop it.'

'But us children run on, you know. So tiresome. Can't be stopped once we start our little games.'

'If the cap fits . . .'

'Oh, it fits, it fits. Trouble is most of us little ones are on the pill nowadays, Hugh. Nicht wahr, Lili?'

'You should discipline her better,' Lili advised.

'No need,' Carla said, smiling. 'I'm off to poison myself in the loo.'

Reviving a school habit, Carla smoked in the lavatory along the hall from her room. Afterwards she weighted the filter tip with a wrapping of soggy tissue and tried to flush it away down the stained lavatory bowl, but the flush was weak and the cistern slow to fill. The soggy ball finally disappeared at her fourth attempt. She felt foolish and slightly angry with herself. Tomorrow, maybe, she'd light up casually in front of Hugh and Lili (Lili could be a buffer) and start acting her age. If he didn't like it he could bloody well send her home. She brightened at the thought. Rubbing Hugh up the wrong way was a passport back to England and Marsha, and to the summer in Geneva they'd planned. She pouted in front of the bathroom mirror, narrowed her eyes sexily.

'So zat vill be ze plan, ja?' she told the mirror huskily. 'Aber zis Lili person, you vill having to vatch her, nein?'

The bathroom was at the far end of the hallway. Between it and Carla's bedroom was a bare stretch of wall about fifteen feet long, broken only by a door marked PRIVAT.

'Ooh,' Carla told an imaginary Lili in her little-girl voice, 'that must mean "Private" in German.' She wondered who lived behind the door: a hotel official of some kind, probably, a desk clerk perhaps. Or the resident Official Snoop. Lili was undoubtedly a snoop for the DDR, a species of commissar, detailed to steer foreigners away from missile sites and things, and confiscate cameras if necessary. Impulsively she tried the handle, ready with the excuse that she thought 'Privat' meant 'Lavatory' (well, it could). Unsurprisingly, the door was locked.

She found Hugh and Lili waiting for her in the lobby.

'Sulks over?' Hugh said.

'Only if I can take my dolly,' Carla answered, and stuck her thumb in her mouth.

A slight summer shower had slicked the cobbles and brought out the city's latent smells, tram oil and brick dust. The sun glinted on windows, the puddles gleamed, the gutters ran rainbows. Some of Carla's claustrophobia lifted.

They took Lili's black Wartburg, a utilitarian little car that buzzed like a motor cycle. While Hugh and the girl shouted at each other in German above the noise, Carla set herself to learning East Berlin's lay-out, trying to keep track of the broad East–West Allees they crossed and re-crossed as Lili swung the car into back streets. She drove, Carla thought, like a car thief: with studied unconcern for the machine or other road users, but competently, her love reserved for the act itself. Her driving was a statement of personality, and it was a strong, masculine technique she had. Carla was awed in spite of herself.

Lili took them north to Pankow first of all, showed them the old village and the Bürgerpark, then drove in a wide half circle through the green outer suburbs of Weissensee, Lichtenberg and Köpenick. The sight of fields and trees relaxed Carla, and there were times during the trip when East Berlin might have been London and not alien at all. Once she caught herself on the verge of asking Lili a question, but swallowed it, not wanting to show too much interest. Besides, the buzzing of the engine had brought back her headache and it suited her to sit quietly back and be passive.

They rested for half an hour at a small airfield, which Lili said was Schönefeld, East Berlin's answer to Tempelhof. Carla smiled at that, glanced once at the field, and said: 'What are we waiting for? Seen it.'

'Perhaps a plane will land,' Lili said.

So they waited in the heat, the Wartburg's black roof soaking up the mid-morning sun. Hugh smoked his pipe and Lili ate dry, un-sweetened biscuits. She offered one to Carla—'Good if you are sick in cars.' No planes landed or took off. Then, when half an hour had passed, Hugh nodded to Lili and said something in German. He opened the window and tapped out ashes. Lili started the car and drove back the way they had come.

They returned to the city via Treptow, approaching from the eastern side this time. When they crossed the Spree over Liebknecht Bridge Hugh pointed out Marx-Engels Platz on the left, and Carla asked who Marx-Engels was to bait Lili. The girl didn't bite, merely smiled an indulgent smile which Carla caught in the rear-view mirror.

'Wasn't Karl Marx a Jew?' she asked innocently.

'Like your Disraeli,' Lili said, and Carla didn't know enough about Disraeli to pursue it.

After parking with the Wartburg's front bumper touching a touring bus, Lili led them through the ornate entrance of the former arsenal, which now housed the Museum of German History. Inside it was spacious and high-ceilinged; fitted carpets, shiny white stands, sterile glass showcases. Modernity to set off antiquity, and the atmosphere of a shrine—hushed, reverent.

Hugh–Lili started at 1789 and made a slow chronological progress. Carla, impatient with the familiar stuff of school history ('blood and iron', 'spiders fascinate me', etc.) wandered decades ahead. Occasion-ally she would double back to check an exhibit, then skip a century in

34

search of something attractive. 'She's like a dog,' Lili observed, watching her. 'Sniff, sniff, your little girl.'

Carla found the section devoted to the Third Reich at the top of a wide staircase. Here she squatted, catalogue in hand, waiting for the others. They came slowly up the stairs, Lili lecturing. 'After 1933,' she was telling Hugh, 'when Hitler became Chancellor, the fascist dictatorship was quickly established. The people were tyrannised in the name of warmongering German imperialism, which led, as previously in the twentieth century, to world war. Here you will see evidence of the vigorous anti-fascism of the KPD, the German Communist Party.'

The displays were of letters, manifestos, tracts, old newspapers. An editorial of *The Red Flag* (an edition of the 'thirties) spoke of the united struggle of the Workers' Party against Hitler. Strange to see that name behind glass in the centre of 'seventies Berlin. Carla leafed through her catalogue, looking for the sensational bits—the SS terror, the beatings, the shootings on the street, the death camps. She couldn't find what she was looking for in the catalogue. She walked on, half expecting to be shocked by something—she wasn't sure what—around the next corner or in the next room; something unnerving, anyway, say Hitler's mummified corpse or his bloody head on a spike, the spike on one of those white, hygienic stands. Something.

They moved on. Lili's monologue droned meaninglessly in her ears, partly in German, partly in English. For her benefit, that. Patronising clever bitch.

Into the war years now. Photographs of people she'd never heard of, people called Thälmann and Pieck and Ulbricht and Weinert. Hitler's photograph too, but the Red-baiting Head of State, not the crowd-puller; Hitler the hypnotist, the beloved Führer was not there. Instead it was communism, communism everywhere: imprisoned communists and martyred communists. Here were the Russians, the once sub-human hordes, an army of rapists, as saviours and liberators; the Nazis a handful of maniacs gripping power with their teeth. It was unreal and more shocking than an exhibition of horrors could have been. A sense of detachment overtook her as she stared into the showcases. In the background she could hear Lili talking to Hugh about the anti-fascist resistance. How prominent the girl made it sound, how fanatical, as if two thirds of Germany had fought in the underground. Yet nothing in the showcases showed what they had been resisting. Where were the baby killers, the butchers, the nightmare people dressed in black, the glossy-booted . . .

'These were a minority,' Lili was saying. 'She has been seeing too many American films.'

Carla felt something snap inside her head.

'Ve haf been vatching you for a long time,' she said to Lili. 'Ve know everysing about your operation. Come vid me, please.'

She clicked her heels together. Her head was throbbing rhythmically now. Hugh and Lili had moved on a few paces, Lili saying: 'She should concern herself with Ireland, or with the American imperialist aggressions in Asia. These are immediate.'

Carla strutted up to them, giggling. She clicked her heels again and shot out her arm in salute.

'Heil Mary! Heil, heil, the gang's all here.'

'Carla,' Hugh said, 'that isn't funny.' Then Lili was asking her why she was so concerned about what happened before she was born, adding something Carla couldn't catch, but which made Hugh smile. They were playing with her. Her hate, fluid, expanded to include them. She heard herself speaking but couldn't understand her own words, and the moment was frightening because she'd only planned part of what was happening—the B-picture Nazi bit, not the other thing, whatever it was, that kept intruding. A smell of cooking came up from somewhere, which made her feel sick. She could feel the wobble beginning in her legs and turned away, looking for a place to sit down. Lili was shouting at her.

'What do you know, little girl from England? History lessons in your school in Sussex or wherever the place is?'

Then it cleared suddenly.

She looked at Hugh and at Lili, around her at the exhibits, felt the soft carpet under her feet. She opened her mouth to speak, but Lili spat: 'Do something about your own doorstep, please, about your Ireland mess.' She had tightened her grip on the yellow shoulder bag, so that for a moment Carla thought she was going to swing at her

36

with it. But Hugh placed a restraining hand on the girl's arm and said something placating to her in German. Lili, bright with fury, stalked off.

The guide was waiting for her at the Fritz Cremer Buchenwald sculpture. Calmer now, she pointed to it.

'What is this? Air?'

Carla saw a small group of figures, sturdily defiant, posing for posterity.

'Where are the toothpicks?' Carla said. 'They look sleek, like they've just had steak for supper.'

Lili gave an unpleasant laugh. 'Your bourgeois child can't be educated,' she informed Hugh. 'Take her out of school and teach her to cut hair.'

Hugh threw back his head and laughed, as if enjoying some fine, private irony. Then he and Lili walked on, talking animatedly in German.

After lunching at a corner café on Unter den Linden, Carla sullenly picking at Rührei mit Schinken, they strolled towards the Brandenburg Gate. Hugh–Lili walked together, Carla a few paces behind. Gradually the gap between them increased. Once, when Hugh stopped for her to catch up, she deliberately sauntered, pretending to be interested in a car showroom of all things. They kept their own pace after that. Hugh–Lili paused to look in the window of a dress shop. Carla halted too. Later, passing the same shop, she noted with satisfaction the Lili-style frumpish clothes it displayed. 'Fifties fashions. She felt ridiculous shadowing the pair of them like a secret policeman bad at the job. It was a child's game, hers was a child's mood. The logic was infantile too, for how else than in Lili's car was she going to get back to the hotel? She hadn't bothered even to check what street the dump was in. In fact, what was the district? Was it Prenzlauerberg? Or had they gone through Prenzlauerberg to somewhere else? And her head was giving her hell. So by degrees, feigning tiredness, she caught them up.

'If you're trying to lose me, okay,' she said to her father. 'Just tell me the fleapit's address.'

37

'We thought you were hanging back,' Hugh said. 'Sulking.'

'Ja, ja. For my next trick . . .'

Lili said, 'You have more choice in the West for shops. The icing is sweetest on a mouldy cake.'

'Marx he say: "Icing sweetest when cake velly mouldy." '

'Grow up, little girl,' Lili told her.

'Drop dead.'

Despite her temper, Lili drove less wildly on the way back, using fewer side roads. The journey seemed very much longer. Carla's headache had developed during the afternoon to the point of nausea. She wondered how Lili would react to her vomiting on the Wartburg's upholstery. She could see Lili pitching her out of the moving car without a qualm. Hugh, of course, would laugh as her skull cracked open on the road. Great joke. She imagined Hugh crossing back to the West weeks later, laughing again when the Chaplin guard asked where his daughter was, Hugh saying something like: "She decided to stay in Prenzlauerberg. She's going to make it her home." The scene grew in her mind. This time Lili was with him, but a much plumper Lili with coarser skin and her hair in a bun, scarcely recognisable as Lili. 'You're big for your age,' Chaplin was saying to her as he checked her passport. Lili answering: 'Don't judge the cake by its icing. I know who I am.' And all of them nodding solemnly as the crash-barrier lifted and the road opened to the free world.

Carla checked herself. The Wartburg had stopped in a familiar street. They were back at the hotel. There was the entrance, and to one side of it, where yesterday there had been corrugated metal cladding, a butcher's shop, open for business. *R. Bruckner: Fleischer*. She could perceive him inside, bristled like a pig, cleaving a leg of pork behind his window. She tried to remember, as she climbed out of the car, what had made her think the shop was abandoned. The metal sheeting had covered the windows, but perhaps that was only a security measure. Meat was a valuable commodity here. No, it had been the signboard. In the gloom last night it had been hard to read, but she could read it clearly enough now. R. Bruckner. Christa Bruckner. She'd got that name from the shop sign without realising it.

There was a strange sensation of floating as she moved away from the car and she wondered, with detachment, if this meant she was about to faint. She hated girls who flaked out suddenly like Victorian heroines, hated the fussing that went on around them, the knowing instructions ('Don't move her', 'Get a glass of water', 'Anyone gone for a doctor?'). Still, if it happened it happened. She found she didn't care one way or the other. Yet she was walking steadily enough. Then she realised what it was that was wrong, not that she was float-ing, but that everyone else was floating. The reason didn't interest her. A dog floated by in slow motion, and stopped to pee a slow, slow, floating yellow stream by the kerb. She heard the car doors slam behind her, glimpsed Bruckner leaving his slab and lumbering slowly, soundlessly towards the shop door, and she couldn't run because someone was standing on her feet, pinning her there until those thick, lard-slimed fingers crushed her arm and the beer-mouth in her ear said, 'And where do you think you're going?'

'Leave me alone,' she heard herself say. 'I'm going in, aren't I?'

Now she found the little room welcoming, its dirt homely. At least that was real. You knew where you were with it. She lay on the bed, having drawn the curtains to keep out the sun, and watched the walls flash different colours. When that stage had passed she was able to enjoy the subdued light and the coolness. From next door, as she dozed, Carla could hear her father's voice and Lili's, distant, resonant. Back at the old itinerary again, discussing places, dates, times. Then another voice, this one harsher-toned, familiar but unrecognised. The two conversations didn't seem to match. She heard Hugh say, 'Yes, I know *Mother Courage*,' and then the other man said, 'Natürlich, Herr Moltke,' but if Moltke was there he didn't speak. Why were they talking at cross-purposes? She drifted into sleep wondering who Moltke might be.

Hugh's tapping woke her up almost immediately. She was dis-oriented. There was too much light and her mouth was dry, her lips sticky. Someone was tapping on the wall to call her, telling her it was late and she was a lazy bitch. And if she didn't get up and work she'd have a strap taken to her arse.

She sat up slowly and swung herself off the bed. Rats in the wall. She waited for several seconds, and when the sound didn't come again she lay back once more and listened to the frantic sounds of her own heart, searching for an unshifting thought to anchor her mind as it rode to sleep.

She had begun to drowse when she heard it again quite clearly. Not the feeble scratching of mice, nor the scrabbling of rats' claws, but a regular hollow tapping. It came from the wardrobe wall, not from her father's wall. Rats didn't tap, either. Or, if they did, not rhythmically. People tapped in that way, so the taps had meaning.

Crossing the room lightly, hardly aware of her feet moving, Carla placed her left ear against the noisy wall. Behind it she could hear faint scraping sounds. She pulled her ear away and sucked her finger. Then, on impulse, she tapped back. There were no answering taps.

The answer came when she was once more in bed and on the threshold of sleep. There was no certainty that she heard them. They might as easily have been dreamed or imagined, those three distinct taps. They sounded as if they had a long way to travel.

Hugh's face was close to hers in the half light when she awoke. It made her start.

'Were you sleeping?' he said.

'No, I was in a coma. Was that you tapping earlier on?'

'Typing?'

'Not typing. Tapping. On the wall.' It could have been Hugh typing at that, she realised. 'Were you typing?'

'No.'

'Then it couldn't have been you typing, could it?'

'What couldn't?'

'Skip it.'

Hugh sat on the bed and pulled out his pipe, twiddled it, put it away again. 'Carla, a word.'

'Antidisestablishmentarianism.'

'All right. Now, seriously.'

'Rats.'

'Look, Carla—

'I mean it. This room's got rats.'

'I'm not talking about rats. I'm talking about your behaviour this afternoon.'

'Oh, that. I was patient, wasn't I? Bet you thought I didn't have it in me. Tell you the truth, I didn't think so either, but I suppose it's because she's so pathetic, really. You have to treat her like a child.'

'Stop playing games, Carla. You know what I'm talking about.'

'Not when you talk in German.'

He sighed. 'Why do you do it? Why can't anyone get through to you?'

'Ah,' she said, 'that's because you don't go about it the right way.'

'All right. Suppose you tell me the right way. I'm willing to try a different approach if it'll help. I feel you're permanently at war with me. And now with Lili. What are we doing wrong, Carla?'

She shrugged. 'Maybe I don't like being treated like a ten-year-old.'

'Then don't act like one.'

'Fantastic repartee. Oh, brilliant barb, that. I'm impaled. Aaah!'

'If you want the proof just listen to yourself now.' He stood up. 'You'd better get out of those jeans if you expect to eat in the dining room. Dinner's in ten minutes.'

'I'm not hungry.'

'Fine. See you at breakfast, then.'

'What am I supposed to do all evening? Train my rats?'

'What is all this about rats?'

She showed him the droppings.

'I'll mention it to Frau Holzbaum,' he said. 'And as for what you're supposed to do to entertain yourself, that rather depends on you.'

Carla sat up. 'Don't follow.'

'It's simple enough. Lili and I are going to see *Mother Courage*—that's a play—at the Berliner Ensemble tonight. Whether you come with us or not depends on whether you're prepared to behave like a young adult. In even simpler terms, Carla, we won't have you showing us up in public again.'

'We? Who's "we"?'

'You know well enough.'

41

'You've got to be kidding.'

'I don't think so. If you want the painful truth, Lili refused at first to consider taking you. I persuaded her to accept your parole.'

'Parole!'

'It means word of honour. Are you going to give it?'

'Tell her she can drop dead. God, parole! Who the hell does she think she is?'

'I'll try and find you something to read, in that case. It'll be in German, of course, but that's what you're here for.'

'I wondered.'

Hugh gave a tired smile. 'There was a more personal reason, but there doesn't seem to be much point in going into that.'

'No there doesn't,' Carla hissed. 'Especially since I won't be stopping long.'

'Oh?' Hugh raised his eyebrows. 'What did you have in mind?'

'Nothing much. Like maybe flying home tomorrow.'

'I don't think so, Carla.'

'I'm not staying here. This place'll drive me out of my mind.'

'Dinner's in . . .' he looked at his watch '. . . eight minutes.'

She picked at the food, her stomach queasy. The sight of Hugh chewing his meat with obvious relish made her heave.

'What's the matter?' he said, watching her.

'Queasy tummy.'

'You're probably hungry and don't know it. Try the cabbage.'

'I hate and detest cabbage.'

'What don't you hate, Carla?'

'Spending the summer in Geneva with my best friend,' she said quickly. Hugh nodded, as if it was an acceptable answer, or the one he'd been expecting.

'It's a rather sterile town,' he said, loading his fork with cabbage. 'What have you decided about tonight?'

'I'm not licking . . . I'm not crawling to chilly Lili, if that's what you're waiting to hear.'

'Fair enough. You can have an early night.'

'Don't be surprised if I'm not here when you get back.'

Hugh looked up. 'Oh, but I would be,' he said. 'Very.'

After that all Carla could hear was the steady slap of his jaws. She watched him with undisguised loathing.

'Schmutz,' said Frau Holzbaum. 'Dirt.'

Carla had just begun a letter to Marsha when Hugh brought the old woman into her room. He showed her the patch of floor where the droppings had been found, and when Frau Holzbaum stood expectantly with her arms folded, refusing to bend a knee, Hugh scooped a sample from the floor. She examined it cursorily, sniffed at it, snorted, and said, 'Schmutz.'

'Es ist nicht Schmutz,' Carla protested. 'Ist Rattedreck.'

'I see you know gutter German well enough,' Hugh said.

'My low-life mentality. Ask her what kind of dirt she thinks that is.'

Frau Holzbaum refused to commit herself. Instead, she scraped up a nailful of grime from the window sill and rolled it between her finger and thumb until it was sweaty-black and elongated. Carla pulled a disgusted face as the old woman held out this ersatz dropping. 'Schmutz.'

'No, kein Schmutz. Nobody's been rolling it.' But Frau Holzbaum was already on her way out. Carla jumped up. 'What about the tapping?'

'Carla, Frau Holzbaum isn't responsible for every sound made in this building.'

'Look, I heard tapping-type sounds through that wall this afternoon. I know they tap phones here, but walls are something beyond. Ist zu brauchig hier,' she said to the woman. 'Hinter den Wand or die Wand, or whatever its blooming gender is. Verstehen Sie? What's "tapping" in German?'

Hugh translated. Frau Holzbaum made the universal I-don't-know gesture and said something to Hugh.

'What she say?'

'She said there's nothing behind that wall.'

'What about that room, then? That door in the hall marked "Privat".'

Frau Holzbaum nodded once, then fished under her clothes and brought out a bunch of heavy keys on a long chain.

'God,' Carla said, 'an ex-jailer. I hope she's ex.'

'She does understand a little English, Carla. You're being offensive.'

'Kommen Sie,' Frau Holzbaum said, beckoning.

They followed her along the hall to the door marked PRIVAT. Frau Holzbaum tried several of the heavy iron keys in the lock, complaining under her breath each time one didn't fit. The fifth key opened the door.

The old woman reached inside and switched on a light. Then she stood to one side and gestured for Carla to go in.

'Why me?'

Hugh had been standing in front of her. Now he moved aside to let Carla see into the room. She saw a cupboard, perhaps three feet deep and six feet wide. There were shelves in it, and on the shelves bottles of cleaning fluid, cans of polish. Two mops and a broom leaned against one wall.

'A broom closet,' Hugh said.

'Ja, ja,' said Frau Holzbaum, and tapped all the walls of the tiny cupboard to show how solid they were.

After re-locking the closet she shuffled back to Carla's room and tapped all the walls there.

'What about behind that thing?' Carla indicated the heavy wardrobe. Frau Holzbaum muttered something in German.

'She says it's fitted. Carla, Lili's waiting downstairs. We'll wait if you want to change.'

'I wouldn't want to be in the way.'

'Don't be absurd.'

Frau Holzbaum was tapping her own head and smiling. Then, leaning over with a surprisingly quick movement, she tapped Carla's.

'Im Kopf,' she said triumphantly.

'She says it's all in your head.'

Carla's room was an oblong, a shoe box. Its long sides were the partition with her father's room, against which her bed stood, and the other, the rat wall, as she thought of it. The heavy wardrobe stood against that. Otherwise the room was sparsely furnished—a dressing table and straight-backed (unmatching) chair under the tall window, the mirror cutting out some of its light; a sagging winged armchair in grey-green brocade shiny with use. There were cigarette burns in its cushion, not surprising as the room had no ashtray.

By eight o'clock Carla had finished her letter to Marsha. It sprawled across six sheets of airmail paper and came nowhere near expressing her feelings. She re-read it with growing dissatisfaction, found it a contemptible essay in self-pity seasoned with flippancy. Somehow the easy wit she and Marsh achieved together at school hadn't been approached in the letter, and she found that ominous. She'd poured herself out on to the flimsy blue sheets, her pen racing to keep up with her thoughts, and it was all there—the hotel, described in techni-colour; the noises in the rat wall; Frau Holzbaum, characterised with a few brilliant pen strokes, and her laconic dismissal of the droppings; her ongoing war against Hugh and his new ally (what she'd called the Anglo-German Pact); the museum—footnotes without history; and in every line her response to the mind-corroding tedium of East Berlin. Yet, despite all this, the letter wasn't 'her', didn't have her sparkle. When she tried to read it with Marsha's eyes she didn't find herself saying: 'Typical Carla,' didn't, in fact, like its pathetic author very much. The last line, for instance—'I've got to get away because I'm not going to be able to stand it here much longer'— that struck a false note. Not because the feeling was false, but because she should have written something more like: 'Having a yuchy time, wish you were here.' Still, she'd sealed the thing now and it was too late to change it. Marsha's reply would take about a week to reach her. She'd know from that how her letter was received.

45

Though it was still light outside, there were so few cars and pedestrians in the street that it might have been the middle of the night. Boredom had already begun to throb in her, an inflammation of the spirit that threatened, if untreated, to spread and turn septic. But there was nothing she could do, nowhere she could go, and she wasn't tired enough to sleep yet. Hugh had been too preoccupied with Frau Holzbaum and with Lili to find her a book to read, even a German book; or else he was deliberately using tedium as an instrument of torture to soften her up and destroy her will. All that showed was how little he knew her.

She settled on the bed and began to leaf through the old Baedeker. There were sixty-four pages of general information about transport, hotels, public holidays and German history. She read selectively at first, her eye seduced by 1936 prices ('persons of moderate requirements' could manage on £1 a day) and some of the more quaintly phrased passages. The Hospize, 'a sort of family hotel or boarding house, often conducted on religious lines', were considered 'very suitable for ladies travelling alone'. That was one for Marsha. She turned back to the beginning and began to read the guide book systematically, totally absorbed by it. It presented a picture of a clean, healthy and strangely old-world society, with special compartments for ladies on the trains and an emphasis on sport. Baedeker made Hitler's Germany sound an attractive place, fresh and virile, full of rosy-cheeked Jungen in shorts eating 'plain, nourishing, and varied' German cooking. It was easy to understand why it had appealed to Miss McClean in her youth.

There was a long section on Berlin, with a pull-out map of the city. She moved to the window to read the small print in better light and to study the map. The Berlin of 1936 was a populous capital city, rich in luxury hotels and expensive restaurants, cabarets, theatres, dance halls and cinemas. Unter den Linden formed the East to West axis of the inner city and extended from the Tiergarten to the Schloss. 'Unbroken lines of motor-cars' flowed along it and through the Brandenburg Gate, where the Wall now ran. Off the Linden was Wilhelmstrasse, containing the Chancellery and the Propaganda Ministry, and Friedrichstrasse, a bustling thoroughfare full of cafés and beer restaurants. There had been an East Berlin then, too, 'almost entirely a factory quarter', though one of its chief sights was the grave of Horst Wessel, the Nazi martyr. And there had been an Adolf-Hitler-Platz and a Hermann-Göring-Strasse. But some things hadn't changed. Tempelhof had been Berlin's airport during the Third Reich too. 'Go by Underground from Friedrichstadt station to Flughafen station in $\frac{1}{4}$ hr.,' Baedeker instructed, 'and thence by a No. 35 tram in 10 minutes.' That confident imperative made Carla smile, and so did the simplicity of 'London ($4\frac{1}{2}$ hrs.)'. Just like that. Four hours and fifty-five minutes and she'd have been home. Before the Wall.

The Baedeker had occupied her for an hour. It was still too early to go to bed. So what was left? How did people in prison pass the time? They made models out of matchsticks and carved beautifully illumin-ated initials in the wall. Or they tapped messages to neighbouring cells.

Tapped on the wall.

She knelt down by the wardrobe, suddenly excited. Rats didn't tap. Prisoners tapped. What if . . . ?

But there was only a broom cupboard behind the wall. She'd seen it.

And a six-foot thickness of masonry between her room and the cupboard.

She tapped hesitantly, holding her breath. When nothing happened she took off her sandal and tapped again with its heel.

Nothing.

At once the room seemed overpoweringly claustrophobic. She had to get out. It was irrational, it was pointless and stupid and oh, yes, juvenile, but she was going.

Now.

Home.

London ($4\frac{1}{2}$ hrs.).

The idea acted on her like a drug. Elated, she began cramming things into her small vanity case (let Hugh send the rest of her stuff on): overnight things, East German money . . . What else? Passport. Frau Holzbaum had that. Something to do with regulations. Where could she go without a passport? For a moment it blocked her, until the next wave of panic broke. And then the passport didn't matter either. All that mattered was getting away, as far away from the hotel,

47

from Berlin, from Germany, as far away as she could. The letter still lay on the dressing table, unstamped. Good. Let it. Tomorrow she'd be telling Marsh in person about this lousy, depressing place. Why not? She wasn't a bloody child, was she? Or a prisoner.

Berlin wasn't the moon.

Berlin wasn't even $4\frac{1}{2}$ hours away from London any longer. More like two. Not the other side of the bloody globe.

For God's sake.

She'd half expected to find the front door blocked, guarded by a Cerberean Frau Holzbaum tapping away at her heads, but the lobby was empty. So was the street, which Carla found a little unnerving. It wasn't nine o'clock yet, on a Wednesday evening. At school they'd be packed round the tv set in the Fifth Day Room, watching some crummy sit-com and laughing in the wrong places. Maybe the East Germans were all watching the box—*Das Kapital* dramatised in twenty-six parts, repeat showing by popular demand. She could imagine them, the beery factory workers of the DDR, leaving the pubs at half eight with a: 'No thanks, Kurt, I'll have the other half-litre tomorrow, my *Kapital* night tonight. Episode Eight, Means of Production. See you.'

Then she realised that she was still standing outside the hotel. The sheet of corrugated iron was back on the butcher shop, nailed over the window with rusty nails, and planks barred the door. She couldn't understand that. The shuttering looked permanent, and that was how it had appeared last night. Carla stepped back until she was standing on the kerb. Now she could see the entire frontage, but there was no signboard, nothing to indicate that the shop would open again in the morning, or what kind of a shop it was, or even that a shop existed behind the cladding. Yet that afternoon, only hours ago, she'd seen him inside, Bruckner, cleaving away at something; heard the bones cracking as the steel thumped rhythmically into the block. That might even have been her tapping sound, Herr Bruckner's cleaver chopping meat in the shop below. She'd *seen* him. She'd even talked to him in that moment when he'd grabbed her as she fainted, though she couldn't remember what they'd said to each other. It puzzled her and frightened her, the whole Bruckner business, but she shrugged it off to make room in her mind for a more immediate problem. Which way to go.

Her knowledge of East Berlin's geography was hopelessly limited. The map in the Baedeker hadn't helped much, except that she'd learned from it that Prenzlauer Allee was north-west of centre. The problem was not knowing exactly where the Wall ran. The Berlin Wall made nonsense of the 1936 map. If Prenzlauer Allee was the nearest station to the hotel she would need to take the Ringbahn to Schönhauser Allee, then change for the U-Bahn. That much would still be true. First, though, she had to find the station. For some reason left felt better than right (fewer shadowy places in that direction now the light was beginning to go), so she turned left and began walking.

It felt peculiar. She put it down to the eerie slap of her sandals on the cobbled road (she avoided the pavements out of habit, the centre of the road being safer for a girl alone in city streets at night), but it was more than that. It was a certainty she felt, even as she put distance between herself and the hated hotel, that she wasn't going to get away. She tried not to think too hard about it, yet the knowledge that she wouldn't make it persisted, weaving like a fighter around her mind's defences, awaiting an opening. She knew about the checkpoint, knew that she would never get beyond it, knew all that but had to try anyway. It was a kind of compulsion, driving her, and that was what felt peculiar. She feared the compulsion more than whatever it was she was running from. It was rational to escape from a place you hated, but irrational and doubly terrifying to run because a small, authoritarian part of your brain insisted that you run without telling you what it shrank from.

And then it felt strange when she turned a corner and found herself unmistakably in Prenzlauer Allee, the Bahnhof visible in the distance. Peculiar because here it was the presence of traffic (albeit light) rather than its absence that seemed eerie and out of place. She was sure they had passed this station in the car last night, on the way to the hotel, and wondered what it was about the way the place had looked then that could have stuck in her subconscious. What was she matching her impression of it now against?

There was a map on the station wall, showing the whole U-Bahn/

S-Bahn system. Carla ran her finger over it and found Prenzlauer Allee. The Ringbahn wasn't marked, so it would have to be the S-Bahn to Schönhauser Allee, change for the U-Bahn, change again for the S-Bahn at Alexanderplatz. She bought a ticket and stood on the platform, waiting. Nobody called out: 'Hey, you, where d'you think you're going?'—nobody pulled at her arm.

The elation was gone now. She felt weary, hopeless, like a rejected child running away, knowing the running away wasn't real or dangerous, that the warm milk and warm bed were still waiting for whenever the game soured and the anger wore off and the stung pride stopped stinging. She wanted to cry, yet loathed herself deeply for feeling that way. But she was going through with it. She wasn't a child. This was a serious attempt. The echo of the words in her brain made her think of suicide, for some reason. There were those who played at it, hoping to be discovered before it was too late, and those who meant it. The rails gleamed below her in the platform's lights. Ah, no. This was a more constructive kind of flight. Also a Serious Attempt.

She was on a train, making good time. Lili had brought them through these north-eastern suburbs only this morning. Greifswalder-strasse. Leninallee. Some of the cars on the avenue had their lights on, she noticed. Zentralviehof. In the failing light the sheds and pens of the vast cattle market, spread along the tracks for fifteen hundred metres. She turned away until they were past, welcomed Frankfurter Allee when it came. Next stop, Ostkreuz.

Ostkreuz!

What the hell was she doing at Ostkreuz? Schönhauser Allee was only one stop, and in the opposite direction from Ostkreuz. She was going away from the centre of the city. Her palms were clammy, the grip of her vanity case sticky with her sweat. She got up and stood by the door, struggling to keep her balance as the train lurched, suddenly desperate for air and security. She was trembling. Ostkreuz was terrifying her. Why?

It had to do with night coming, darkness coming. The sky threat-ened and Ostkreuz threatened shadows; it was all looming buildings, a maze of criss-crossing railway tracks, a nest of terrors. Carla reacted to it from her depths, wanting to break and run. Somehow the place was more than she could bear, it stripped the years off her until she was very small again and dreaming she was lost. Black stone, black brick, high walls, narrow ways, chimneys: a set from nightmare. Its image was a factory at night, deserted, not a light in the place, but with all its machines going in the dark.

She stood on the platform trying to fight the surging panic that rose like vomit in her throat, craving the safety of a small room to shut herself away in. She felt she had arrived at the destination of the lost. There were no exits, no words to explain what she felt as the train pulled out without her and left her alone, night coming.

So she clutched her case and began to run.

And her own running startled her as she clacked in her sandalled feet through the quiet of Rummelsburg, past the shunting yards; and the sound of herself running made her run faster still.

She began to whimper. The buildings she passed seemed to contain no people. But was it people she wanted? It was to run far and fast, to get away that she wanted.

Then the darkness came down. *Es dunkelt* . . . , the phrase from the poem, ran through her mind like a leitmotif, passing the same point in her brain every few milliseconds. And suddenly this was the horror that surpassed all other horrors, the dark, being caught in the dark.

There was a lighted doorway ahead of her, up six stone steps. She threw herself at the door with all her weight and hammered.

Perhaps she screamed too, but she was hammering, oh God, she was hammering for her life.

A family took her in, the kindly family of German folk tale. A grey-haired man with thick, yellowed fingers, who smelled of iron filings and wore a boiler suit. The Frau (Carla expected him to address her as 'wife') thrust a cup of hot milky coffee into her hands and spoke soothingly to her in German while she sipped it. There was a small boy there too, who looked at her with undisguised curiosity. Carla smiled at him. When she leaned forward and said 'Hello,' the boy said: 'Amerikanisch?' She shook her head. 'Englisch,' she said, and the boy turned and walked away, disappointed.

51

Carla and the boy's mother (no, grandmother, as in folk tales) laughed at that, the laughter dispelling what was left of her nightmare experience. She felt foolish and embarrassed now. She wanted the scene to disappear, to be replaced by something familiar. It was an uncomfortable feeling to have fled like a child before phantoms of the dusk and to be succoured by this ordinary family.

And on *Kapital* night, of all nights. She giggled at the thought, looking around for the television set, but there was none.

They delayed her when she tried to leave. If she'd had the language she could have explained that her panic had been unaccountable, but without it she was reduced to lunatic shakings of the head and a stream of English that puzzled the Germans. 'Ich bin nicht hysterisch,' she said, which they seemed to understand, so she supposed that unlikely word existed.

Then, when the Volkspolizei arrived, her panic returned. 'Nein, nein,' she found herself saying over and over, and 'Es dunkelte und ich war verloren.' The policemen nodded, without understanding.

She was taken in a police car to a disinfectant-smelling building and placed in a bare, overbright room while telephone calls were made.

Hugh arrived an hour and a half later. Something about his look made Carla's stomach flutter. There was no relief in it, no obvious concern or anger. He gave her instead a hard, expressionless stare, like a mask.

'Were you attacked?'

'No.'

'They want to know if someone tried to rob you,' he said tonelessly. Carla shook her head. She had no language to communicate with Hugh either. 'What were you running from?' he asked. She shrugged.

He took her back to the hotel in the red Volkswagen. Not a word passed between them on the way.

She was too troubled to sleep.

First there had been her attempts to reconstruct and make sense of the happenings at Ostkreuz. She'd drawn a blank. Labelled 'mental aberration' the evening had been finally tucked away into a corner of her crowded mind. Then her thoughts, as she lay in bed, had turned to Hugh. Hugh was the real puzzle. She'd expected threats, recriminations, an outburst. Instead, he'd driven her back in silence, deposited her in her room and said: 'It's late. You can sleep in tomorrow.' Afterwards she'd heard him walking back down the hall, then, faintly, the clump of his feet on the stone stairs. Half an hour later he'd gone into his room, where he'd moved about for several minutes before getting into bed. And now the very thought of him was making her shudder.

In the end she had to get out of bed to have a smoke. As a precaution against discovery by Hugh she had wedged the straight-backed chair against his door, pushing it up under the handle. Any sideways movement of the chair under pressure would be prevented by the foot of her bed. Its head end was squeezed between Hugh's wall and the dressing table, an arrangement that also gave her a ready-made bedside table. In fact, the room seemed quite well planned, tidy if poky. She was now sure there had been a woman's touch in its planning, though she doubted that it had been Frau Holzbaum's. Unfortunately, there was nothing she could do to secure the hall door. The only item of furniture heavy enough to use as a barricade was the wardrobe, and to shift that—if she could—would have made too much noise. Besides, the old biddy had said it was a fitment, and the thick line of grease between it and the wall made it hard to tell.

She was sitting as close as she could get to the half-open window. She had to lift herself out of the low armchair to flick ash through the window and had to make the same movement, leaning forward, to exhale each lungful of smoke. The night being windless, none blew back in. It was relaxing, sitting in the security of her little room, sucking the smoke into her lungs. She felt at peace. After the cigarette sleep would be welcome. Her thoughts wandered.

She remembered the tapping, and her theory that what she'd heard might have been Bruckner cleaving meat below. Otherwise there were only two explanations which seemed at all reasonable. And both were unreasonable. So much for logic.

One was that the sounds (if, indeed, she hadn't imagined them) had originated on another floor of the building and by some fluke acoustic effect were distorted so that they seemed to come from behind her wall. The other, much more fanciful, depended on a phantom tapper solemnly communicating from inside the broom closet—a cleaner, say, or Frau Holzbaum, going into the cupboard to tap away for Carla's benefit. Which, considering the thickness of that wall, would mean that the cleaning woman (did they have domestics in proletarian democracies?) or Frau H or a giant rat would have to be pounding away in there with a sledge hammer.

And what for?

She tried to recall the sequence of events, though the incident was vague, only half remembered. The tapping had woken her up. She had gone to the wall to listen. Had she tapped back, or was that a fantasy? And in bed, afterwards, had the sounds come again? The episode was fuzzy and dreamlike, like so much else that had happened recently. That worried her. She immediately tucked the worry away and threw her cigarette stub out of the window without bothering to check whether anybody was passing below. It didn't seem to matter.

Then she carried the armchair, struggling with its bulk, to the rat wall and sat with her ear against the wallpaper.

What if—she shivered a delicious shiver—the wall was hollow?

What if—da-da! Descending chords—someone was behind the wall trying to contact her? No, seriously. What if? Who? Some pervert, maybe, getting his thrills by tapping obscene messages in Morse code? She smiled. Poor perv, tapping dirty messages that couldn't be understood. Hugh in a stained raincoat, doing his Jekyll and Hyde act. She suppressed a giggle, then padded across the room to listen at Hugh's wall. Nothing going on behind there. Just Hugh dreaming of Lili. Another giggle rose in her throat. The strain of standing there in the dark stifling laughter made her want to pee. She crossed her legs and bit on a finger. A picture popped into her head of Hugh smiling beatifically, dreaming of darling Lili. She saw him supine and naked, erect, his lips working in his sleep, and a naked Lili emerging like a sexy genie from a bubble inside the dreamer's head. Wiggling out.

Stroking him. Whispering sweet dialectical nothings in his ear. Yuch!
She banished the image, disgusted by her own imagination.

Back to the rats.

Somewhere in the hotel a baby was crying. She listened to it, waiting for the sound of a door opening on one of the other floors, footsteps, soothing mother sounds. But the baby went on crying, the
cries turned to screams, then abruptly it stopped. Carla strained to
catch the mother's voice, but it was too far away to be audible. Probably top floor, too far off. Pity, a lullaby would have soothed her too.

Back to the rat wall, Carla. Now if she still had her Girl Guide
Morse she'd be able to play the perv's own game and tap English
obscenities. They'd be mutually stymied. The problem was that all
she knew in Morse was the usual dit-dit-dit, da-da-da, dit-dit-dit, the
international distress signal. Well, why not? Hers was a kind of
distress situation.

To save her knuckles she fetched her hair brush from the dressing
table. She began tapping S.O.S., exaggerating the da's to distinguish
them from the dit's. After each message she would stop and listen.
She was listening for tapping noises, so at first she didn't hear anything. Then, after her fourth S.O.S., something. So faint she could
hardly be sure of it. An echo? Seriously, she'd heard something just
now from the other side of that wall. Not tapping, more of a scraping
sound. Rats were a real possibility. She tapped again, listened again.

Scrape, scrape.

She jerked back from the wall, the armchair with her, rolling
squeakily on its casters. Oh, Jesus, there was someone behind there.

The really strange thing, though, the fantastically odd thing was
that she was totally calm. Once the shock wore off she wasn't afraid.
If that wasn't weird, what was? Because she ought—Carla who ran
from shadows in the suburbs—ought to be terrified out of her skull
when a maniacal pervert tapped and scraped on her wall in the dead
of night. Now that *was* a classic nightmare situation. She began to
think through her next moves with detachment. First, find a way in.
Whoever was there was probably not in the broom closet but in a
secret passage or something—God, vintage girls' adventure stuff, this:
'I say, you lot, look what I've found. A secret passage. I say, let's

see where it goes.' She chased away the image. No, think of it as a priest-hole. All right, so Carla finds a priest-hole. Carla tunnels in, comes face to face with a knife-wielding maniac in the pitch dark. Maniac slits Carla's throat. End of Carla. Hugh throws a party, adopts Lili as daughter-mistress and takes her away from all this. Crazy.

She lit another cigarette with slightly trembling fingers.

Where was she? Oh, yes, having her throat cut. Not convincing, her tapper-scraper didn't sound aggressive enough, maniacal enough. She'd rather think of him (or her) as a poor, lonely sod who needed companionship. Someone like herself.

She began to sound the wall systematically with the handle of her hair brush. Masonry. Masonry. Frau Holzbaum had been right, bless her knickers, it was solid all the way. So that left the built-in wardrobe, too heavy to shift on her own. On the other hand, nothing ventured
. . .

She braced herself against the wall, legs well apart, and had begun trying to move the heavy old thing when a series of sounds, sensations of movement jerked her around. She felt a draught. The hall door was open. Someone was in her room, crossing the floor. Oh, God.

'The midnight tapper, I presume,' Hugh said. His voice was without humour.

'God, you scared the daylights out of me.'

'Do you know what time it is, Carla?'

'I heard it again,' she said. 'That noise.'

'Carla, I'm getting very tired.'

'Well, it's pretty late,' she said, warming to the situation.

'I don't want to play word games with you.' He was sniffing. 'Have you been smoking?'

'Smoking?'

'Smoking. Smoking cigarettes. Have you?'

'What if I have?' Under cover of a cough she dropped the cigarette to the floor and shifted her weight, seeking it with her slippered foot.

'Where are they?'

'Do you have to be so heavy about it?' She attempted a nonchalant yawn, but cringed when he stepped closer.

'I said where are they?'

'Go to hell.'

He slapped her face. She didn't move. She stared at him disbelievingly.

'You've had that coming,' Hugh said.

Carla was biting her lip. Her legs were shaking. The shock had dissolved her.

'I hate your guts.'

'Now, where are they?'

'On the dressing-table. And I'm going home tomorrow. You can't stop me so don't think you can. I'm going first thing in the morning.' She bit off this last word, her voice breaking. The bastard, the fat ugly old bastard. Let him go, please let him go so she could think about it without him being there. She'd die before she cried in front of him.

He was fumbling to find the cigarettes in the dark. She heard the pack slide momentarily as he brushed against it with his fingers, the slight crackle of the cardboard as he picked it up, the rattle of her matches, pocketed.

'Any more?'

'I can buy more.'

'I wouldn't if I were you.'

Anger filled her face with blood. She felt she would have given her life for the strength to spring at him and choke him. Was that the blind, irrational rage that madmen felt, and was that what gave them superhuman strength?

Her voice came out hoarse. 'I told you,' she said, 'I'm going back in the morning. You'll have to kill me to stop me.'

What sounded like a chuckle came out of the gloom. 'You'd need a visa.'

'I'll get one.'

'You've got one,' Hugh said. 'But it's joint. You can't leave without me. You've had a busy evening, Carla. Get some sleep.'

Suddenly her tiredness was overwhelming. A mass of things—panic, his slap, this new knowledge—leapt on her at once, a live weight, pulling her down like dogs. She felt the wall at her back and the floating sensation, fleetingly, as she slid to a sitting position. Then the cool lino touched her face, and she was being half-lifted, half-dragged. She heard his laboured breathing, felt the softness of the bed under her, the tightness of covers pulled over her legs.

Then a door closed.

And it seemed that she was trapped in a dark, damp place, hammering to be let out, hammering to let them know she was alive and terrified of the dark and of the silence. And though she knew it was a dream there was no escape from the dream, no escape except death, which would end neither the darkness nor the silence, only the awareness. Perhaps not even the awareness.

So this was what it felt like to be dead.

FOUR

Frau Holzbaum came in with a tray, set it down, went back out, came in with a chamber pot, opened the curtains. The sudden light made Carla's eyes water. She dabbed at them with her bare forearm. She registered an overcast day, the pot, a boiled egg and a roll, coffee, the drab brown of Frau Holzbaum's dress (definitely her colour).

What the hell was going on?

'Was ist los?' she said.

Frau Holzbaum muttered something on her way out. Before Carla had time to call to her the woman had closed the door. She was half out of bed when she froze at the sound of a key being turned in the lock. She prodded her slow senses. It just wasn't happening. The old bitch had locked the bloody door, locked her in.

She tried Hugh's door. That was locked too. No, this was unreal.

Carla wanted to laugh at the absurdity of it, the fantastic, Gothic absurdity of it. It was horror film stuff, pure corn. Creaky doors and maniacal laughter from the Locked Room. Frau H was the Sinister Wardress. She and Marsh broke up watching stuff like this in the Day Room, but that was tv and this was *happening*. And last night—the scraping behind the wall, Hugh pussyfooting in on her, her flaking. Now being the Prisoner of Prenzlauer was too much, too funny to be real.

She tried a burst of maniacal laughter and liked the effect. Maybe she'd try that on Frau Kopf later, when she came back; if it got her committed she couldn't be much worse off.

Anyway, there was breakfast. Boiled egg and coffee wasn't the stuff of Edgar Allan Poe remakes. Drugged wine was what Vincent Price and Christopher Lee went in for.

Frau Holzbaum had muttered something about 'Krank'. They were treating her as a bed-case, then. Chamber pot and all. That was standard horror movie treatment, too—'You are not well, my dear, you must rest.' What was that Hitchcock thing where he put poison in her milk? She sniffed at the coffee. It smelled like coffee. She drank some. What the hell did poison taste like, anyway?

Hugh's note was tucked under the egg plate. Carla read it with masochistic delight and decided it deserved to be framed as a little three-line classic. On hotel notepaper Hugh had written: 'Humboldt University wouldn't interest you anyway. Have the day in bed. Hugh.'

She wouldn't have put it past him to have added a P.S. about locking her in for 'her own safety'. Typical Hugh that would have been. But there was no P.S. on the back. No reference either, she noted, to last night's melodrama. That was what it had been, she now realised. Brutish father slaps daughter's face. Daughter declares undying hatred then faints away to be carried to bed by remorseful papa. Beauty and the Beast—Victorian style.

She started on the egg. Thin yolk, and—Yuch!—the white was still snotty. She pushed it away.

She ate the roll and drank the coffee, remembered what had happened to her cigarettes and groaned. Now that was a refinement. Torture. Locking her in a crummy room all day without cigs. Maybe her pet pervert smoked. She could cadge one off him. A drag, a drag, my virginity for a drag. Or the window. She still had the window. If she leaned out and called to some passing Kraut: 'Hilfe Mir. Ich bin Gefangene. Mein Vater hat mich im Zimmer geschlossen.' Fat chance. Of course, it was possible that Frau Kopf hadn't locked her in on Hugh's orders (who was he to give her orders?), but had done so absent-mindedly. It was a small possibility, easy enough to check. All she need do was hammer on the door until Frau Sinister came and ask her sweetly to unlock the door. Somehow she didn't think so. Or why provide her with a potty? No, Hugh had ordered it, all right. That was a lot of weight for a foreign visitor to swing in the DDR. What could he have told the old cow? Easy. 'My daughter's a raving lunatic.' Frau Kopf would go for that. Actually, more likely he'd said she was delirious or something, might run out with the screaming hab-dabs again and get herself under a tram this time. Either would work. The second was more likely, though.

She played with another idea. That of stationing herself behind the door when Frau Holzbaum came back for the tray, to empty the pot, to bring lunch, whatever—and then either bashing her head in or slipping nimbly past her. Mind, the old cow could move. She'd moved pretty fast yesterday. Like the fairy-tale princess hexed into a crone, she was probably a DDR star gymnast doing spare-time old biddy work and made up to look the part. And Lili was probably her sister.

The take-Frau-Holzbaum-by-surprise ploy was short-lived. As soon as Carla's frantic imagination took her beyond the hotel she realised that the furthest she could hope to get, even with a following wind, would be Checkpoint Charlie. Hugh had the exit permit, visa, everything except her passport. She shuffled possibilities. Pick the lock of Hugh's door or force it? But what if he had the visa on him, as he surely would? Then the sickening memory of what he'd said in the night jolted her. It was a joint thing, like a joint passport. He would be able to leave without her. She couldn't go without him.

Adopting a half-lotus position on the bed, Carla tried to order her thoughts. The main problem was the pace at which everything was moving. It seemed there was no time to assimilate one crazy status quo before a still crazier one usurped it. It was like trying to adjust to the whims of a succession of lunatic emperors; no, more like Alice uselessly applying logic to the looking-glass world. There was still the tapping problem to be solved, but that was academic and pure Form One stuff by comparison with the getting-out-of-East-Berlin problem. She considered the thought that had just passed through her mind. Getting-out-of-East-Berlin. How bloody juvenile that sounded. As if it was something actually open to solution by her, when hard-nosed professionals were shot every day trying to crash that border. Yet here she was solemnly, fatuously thinking about it as a possibility. Carla Martin, Girl Agent. Read next week's *School Friend* to find out what happens.

She checked her watch. 10.05. Frau Holzbaum had been gone about an hour. Chances were the old girl wouldn't be back until lunch time, not before noon at the earliest and perhaps later than that. Which gave Carla about two free hours. Time enough to sort out one puzzle at least.

There was a different feel about her room in daylight. Outside people were passing by, hanging out washing, stopping to chat. Cyclists trundled past on the cobbles and occasionally one of those motor-cycle-cars buzzed by under the window. From a distance (Prenzlauer Allee?) came the subdued sounds of heavier traffic. Her theories and concerns of last night seemed fevered now, the night-fears of a child. And didn't Death-Watch beetles make tapping noises? Whatever the answer was, it would be something as mundane as that, you could bet.

Carla ran a fingernail, then a hairclip, down the line between the wardrobe and the wall. A thick paring of grease came away. She then traced the wardrobe's entire outline (standing on a chair to reach the highest places), stopping from time to time to clean the hairclip, until its meeting point with the wall was sharply defined.

She tapped, tentatively.

Nothing.

Now what she needed was something thin but strong to prise with. She looked around the room. Coffee spoon? She tried it but it began to bend immediately and wasn't thin enough, anyway. A screw-driver would have been perfect. Next time she'd pack a tool kit, complete with jemmy and skeleton keys. Nail-file too bendy. Scissors?

Scissors. She had a pair of stainless steel nail scissors in her vanity set, thin-bladed but strong. Using these (closed, to get the strength of both blades) as chisel and a boot heel as mallet, Carla drove a wedge between the wall and the back of the wardrobe, on the left-hand side about half-way up. The next step was to slip her stainless steel ball pen into one of the finger loops, so that it could serve as a tommy bar. With this leverage she managed to exert enough force to flex the heavy piece of furniture momentarily away from the wall; long enough for her to catch a glimpse of lighter wallpaper behind it.

As expected. No surprises there.

The second she relaxed her pressure on the scissors the wardrobe snapped back into place. Something was holding it to the wall. End of game, then. The wardrobe was, as Frau H had said, a fixture.

There was only one other approach possible, and that meant open-ing the wardrobe. She broke into a sweat at the thought of it. A nest of rats, lying in years of accumulated filth, pin-point eyes in the dark interior. Come on, Carla, you'd have heard them squeaking and scrabbling about in there. Dead rats, then. No, they'd have stunk the place out. So what was it she was afraid of?

The dark. What she had in mind entailed standing inside the wardrobe, in the stuffy dark, in an upright coffin. Last night's business had to do with darkness too, but it was being lost in the dark she had feared then. You couldn't get lost in a wardrobe. She imagined Marsha saying, 'Well, what happened when you opened the wardrobe?' and herself saying, 'I didn't actually open the wardrobe,' and for no obvious reason that seemed to make it all right. She wrenched open the door.

It smelled musty, of old wood.

She flicked on her night-light. A scrap of brown paper lay on the floor. Half a dozen wooden coat hangers dangled from the rail.

With the door wide open the wardrobe wasn't uncomfortably dark or stuffy. Carla now used the scissors to scrape away at its wooden back panel, peeling off the grime with both points. She started high up, standing on her toes to reach the top left corner, where logically she might expect to find a screw. How I Spent My Summer Holiday. 'I spent my summer holiday in a large wardrobe in East Berlin, scraping the dirt off with my nail scissors . . .' She smiled to herself, feeling ridiculous. Oh, for a camera. 'That's me, in the wardrobe, making my miniature square search.' She was scraping two-inch squares, moving systematically down and to the right. The first two squares were hard going. She came out of the wardrobe after the first one to stretch and massage her right arm. She did the same after the second.

The third square, easier to reach, took less time.

The fourth square contained a screw head.

The head was evenly rusted, its slot burred a little. It had been there a long time.

Carla stopped to think about that. If the screw (and presumably at least three other screws in the remaining corners) had been there long enough to rust in position, it implied that nobody could have got behind the wall via her room. Therefore, logic said, there was no point in trying to get the screws out. True, yet she recognised rationalisation when she heard it. She knew there was no way she could get those screws out, and so she was justifying not trying. No go, Carla, she told herself. It was already nearly half past ten. If nothing else, the exercise was at least passing time. Back to work.

She experimented with the scissors as a screwdriver (too thin, wrong shape), the head of her vanity case key (also too thin), the coffee spoon again (flimsy—aluminium), then with various coins. None of the German coins were thick enough; nor was an English sixpence or 2p piece. The slot of the screw was unusually wide, in spite of the burring. A 10p piece fitted, but leverage was poor. Best of a bad lot was her lucky 50p, the mad money she kept in a separate compartment of her purse. The same thickness as the 10p coin, this, with its irregular heptagonal shape, offered a much better grip. Carla found that by wrapping the portion of the coin she gripped with a folded-over glove (thin, supple leather), she could exert considerable force with it. She used the left glove and wore the right to give her fingers extra protection. And by bringing the straight-backed chair into the wardrobe and standing on it, she was also able to improve her leverage.

At first she worked in her nightdress, but her exertions in the confined space soon soaked her in sweat. She changed the wringing nightdress for a light cotton frock, resenting the time this took, checking her watch three times in five minutes.

For all their rustiness, the screws yielded to her pressure. There were only four of them, but getting them out was a slow business, not becoming easier—as Carla had hoped—the further out the screws came. They continued to squeak as she unscrewed them, rusty along shank and thread, and the last quarter inch of each screw required as much effort as the first. They were 50 millimetre screws.

The first one came free at 10.45, the second at 10.55. Carla was acquiring technique but losing the feel of her fingers. Bathed in sweat again, her dress stained with it in places, she worked the third screw loose just after eleven o'clock and gave herself a ten-minute break. She lay on the bed, chilling rapidly, light-headed with exhaustion.

She was unsteady on her feet when she returned to the wardrobe, and grateful that the last screw was in the bottom right-hand corner. She sat on the wardrobe floor to reach it, leaning against a side panel.

This screw was badly burred. The coin slipped out of the slot with infuriating regularity, and once Carla ripped her hand on a sliver of jagged steel. She bound the cut hastily with a tissue, frowning at the blood which soaked through. The last turn of thread squeaked out at 11.33.

Now there was a time problem. Any time after midday was technically lunch time (she wasn't certain of the hotel's meals schedule), so all she could count on was another half hour without interruption. Time enough to pull the wardrobe away from the wall, but not enough to explore whatever was behind it. There was also the point of no return to be considered, once she'd hauled the thing out. Would she have enough warning of Frau Creep's approach to be able to get it back in time?

Or was something else holding her back? She thought about it while changing clothes again—this time into jeans and a blouse. God, by the time this was over she'd have gone through her entire wardrobe. She giggled at the pun. She tried to analyse her feelings and realised that she was afraid of finding nothing behind the wardrobe and equally afraid of finding something. Anything. In a locked room there were no flight options. The thought chilled her.

She licked at the brown-red stain on the tissue over her hand, then jerked it away. It revealed an inch-long gouge across her thumb, between the joints. It began to throb as she looked at it.

Frau Holzbaum came back shortly before twelve. Carla had begun levering the wardrobe away from the wall. The scissors-and-ball-pen technique gave her finger space. Now she had her left hand between the wall and the back of the wardrobe, her left thigh against the wall as anchor, and was push-pulling the thing with the weight of her body, when she heard Frau Holzbaum's footsteps outside. She had time to jump away and turn towards the door before the old woman was in the room.

'Mittagessen,' Frau Holzbaum said, looking around. The wardrobe was only fractionally out of position. Close scrutiny couldn't miss it, but a glance would. Frau Holzbaum's glance passed over it and settled on the chamber pot. She pointed at it.

'It doesn't need emptying,' Carla said. Frau Holzbaum came for a closer look and, finding the pot empty, nodded. She was now several feet from the door. Carla was slightly closer to it. If she took the old bat by surprise, if she was just slightly faster . . . But Frau Holzbaum had already turned back. She stood by the door, gripping the handle.

'Mittagessen,' she said again. 'Eine Halb-Stunde. Sie wollen Fleisch?'

'No, no meat. Kein Fleisch. Warum bin ich in meinem Zimmer geschlossen?'

Frau Holzbaum left without answering.

She was back thirty-five minutes later with a lunch tray. Thin-looking broth of some kind with bits of cabbage floating in it, a dish of mashed potato with an egg on top, another roll, a glass of water. Again Carla asked why she had been locked in. All Frau Holzbaum would say was 'Sie sind krank, ja?'—You're ill, aren't you?

Carla drank less than half the soup, ate the roll, and two forkfuls of mashed potato (leaving the egg untouched, careful not to break its yolk). She drank the water greedily and wished there had been more of it.

At 12.44 she put her weight to the wardrobe again. Five minutes later she could get her entire forearm behind it. By one o'clock she could crouch behind it. She fetched her light, the scissors, the hair-brush and made herself comfortable.

The light showed her a rectangle of new-looking wallpaper, white, criss-crossed by black lines forming diamond shapes. The motif, in red, appeared in every fourth diamond. Carla checked the pattern in another part of the room and found it was the same, though un-identifiable through the dirt unless you knew what to look for. So the wardrobe had been screwed to the wall a long time ago and just after a re-decoration. It was a new fact, though not a particularly interesting or suprising one. Still, it was something a less enterprising girl wouldn't have established. What was next? To strip the paper? Irrational, but she didn't want to tear off the clean paper. Once the furniture was back in place and screwed to the wall there was no chance of her vandalism being discovered. It wasn't that. She sup-

66

posed it was a habitual neatness that made her balk. Instead of picking up the scissors she reached for the brush. Then she began tapping.

An area—she sounded it out—roughly half the size of the wardrobe, narrower and shorter, perhaps six feet high by three feet wide. Wooden-sounding. Hollow-sounding. Like hardboard or ply. Definitely not masonry. An area beginning at floor level, door-shaped. She felt herself shaking. She put down the hairbrush with exaggerated care, suddenly afraid to make a sound. Ah, this was fear, the genuine article. Where had it been hiding all along? She stared at the clean patch of wall, half expecting it to rip apart as someone burst through from the other side, some snarling, foaming homicidal maniac with a meat cleaver in his hand. Oh, God. She inched back, leapt out of the space and ran to the window. She opened it as wide as she could and leaned out, breathing deeply. A small boy passed below, looked up at her, waved. She smiled and waved back. A Hausfrau came out of the hotel carrying a bloody parcel—no, from the butcher's shop, of course. Normality. Bustle. Night-fears again, Carla? By daylight?

Decisively, without thinking, without giving herself time to object or her imagination time to be inventive, she crouched behind the wardrobe again and picked up the nail scissors. With the double point she probed the line where the hollowing soundings had started, identified it, and began slitting the paper. The scissors penetrated over an inch. Single-bladed, two inches, until stopped by the thickening where the blades were riveted together. Using the cutting edge of one blade, Carla traced the outline of her sounding—yes, a door. Then she pulled at the ragged edges of the paper, tearing them away in fine strips and fist-sized sheets. Underneath was a kind of board, manila-coloured, possibly hardboard. All right, so how did it open? There was no handle, apparently no hinges. Did it slide, as secret panels traditionally did (usually you had to lean by accident on a loose brick)? She leaned on parts of the surrounding wall. The panel stayed put. She tried pushing it, then levering it with the scissors. It wasn't nailed, clearly, because she could feel a good bit of give in it. Perhaps if lifted out. She tucked the fingers of her right hand into the crack at the right of the panel, her left hand on the other side. Gripping with her nails, she pulled sharply. The panel (light, very like hard-board) came suddenly free, tipping Carla into a sitting position. She stared into the dark space revealed, shrank at the smell that came from it, a disgusting stench of rot and age, but with something else in it. Sour milk? Bad meat? Her stomach was suddenly light, its contents loose and floating, beginning to rise. She breathed through her mouth, not wanting to leave the wall now she was so close to finding what-ever was behind it.

She shone the night-light into the cavity.

Something in a heap. Flesh-colours, whites, a flash of green. Oh, God, a corpse. A putrefying corpse. She clapped her hand over her mouth. She swung the light in an arc. Mostly patches of dark in different shades, from charcoal grey through various dark browns to absolute mind-melting black. She swung the light back again, higher this time. Had that been a papered wall? She tried to follow the same arc back, but failed to find whatever it was. Switching off the lamp, she let out her breath. She had been holding it, unconsciously, for almost a minute. It was impossible for her to breathe shallowly now, to suck in only small amounts of the vile air. She was gulping in great draughts of it, retching dryly. God, her soul for a cigarette now, the beautiful, fragrant blue smoke of one in her rebelling lungs.

Then Carla became aware of another impression from the priest-hole, cavity, whatever it was. Light. The very faintest quantity of white light, only discernible at all because of its contrast with the darkness it pierced. The light came in thin, pale lines, as if seen through clouded glass. It triggered off a memory. The boarded-over window she'd noticed on arriving two nights ago (only two?). She made an effort to visualise the facade as she'd seen it then—first floor, to the left of the entrance, directly above the abandoned butcher's shop. That would have made sense. A disused meat store-room, complete with decomposing carcases, over a disused shop. The air from the cavity, foul as it was, suggested that. And it was cool, too, though not refrigerated. The only snag was that the shop was in use. She kept coming back to that. Why the metal cladding if the place was a going concern?

She turned over possibilities in her mind even as she crawled, push-

68

There was no sound of a key turning in the lock. The door simply opened. Hugh put his head round it, knocking at the same time, then walked into Carla's room followed by Lili.

'Decent?' he said.

'Disappointed?' Carla answered, surprised that he was so cheerful. She had changed back into the nightdress and was lying on the bed. Lili, too, seemed unusually bright. She pulled out the straight-backed chair and arranged herself on it, smoothing the calf-length skirt of her black suit. Hugh sat on the end of the bed. Carla said, 'Isn't anyone going to ask me how I like prison life? I might want to complain about the food or something.'

Hugh rubbed his hands together. 'Nice restful day in bed. We've been envying you, haven't we, Lili?'

'Have you occupied yourself?' the guide said.

'On the go non-stop. It's such a fascinating place, this room. I mean it looks like a poky little hole, but you wouldn't believe how much there is to explore.'

She watched them carefully for a reaction. Hugh shifted his position slightly.

'Sorry I couldn't find you a book.'

'It's okay. Told you, I explored.'

Lili said, 'Did you find anything interesting?'

'Oh, yes. Fascinating. See if you can guess.'

'You seem perky enough,' Hugh said. 'How's your appetite?'

'Didn't she report yet?'

'Sorry. Who?'

'Frau Turnkey. I'd have thought you'd have got her report first.'

'Come on,' Hugh said, 'what is all this?'

'I mean, maybe I should see the prison doctor or something.'

'A doctor would be helpful,' Lili said, turning over Carla's nail

73

scissors. 'Made in West Germany. I thought she had tough nails.'
She laughed.

Hugh said, 'All right, I give up. Somebody explain the references
to prison, please.'

Carla sat up. 'You've got to be joking.' She pointed to the chamber
pot. 'What's that for?'

'We thought you might not feel up to going to the bathroom.
I'm sorry if it's a little indelicate, Carla.'

'That "we" again.'

'I discussed it with Lili. Lili's very concerned about you.'

'Yes,' Lili said, crossing to the armchair. 'Why does she keep her
lovely clothes on a chair? She has an armoire.' The girl started rum-
maging through Carla's clothes like someone at a jumble sale.

'I haven't got round to putting them away. And stop changing the
subject. I want to know why I was locked in.'

Hugh made a puzzled face. 'Your door wasn't locked.'

'Not when you came in. Frau Thing must have sneaked back and
unlocked it when I was . . . when I was sleeping.'

The realisation froze her. When she was in the cold room. That
was why she hadn't heard the door being unlocked. What if the old
bat had looked in? God, she must have looked in. So she knew. And
Hugh knew. And all this was a game because the whole bloody
hotel knew about the cold room and what was in it, and for some
reason she wasn't supposed to know that they knew . . .

'You look flushed, Carla,' Hugh was saying.

It was like a chess game. Then what was her best move? To play
along or bring the whole thing into the open? Prisoners, she remembered from her thrillers, gained advantage by hiding their
strength.

'There's no air in here,' she said.

'Feel up to dinner?'

She shook her head. 'Could I have a tray again? I could fancy some
hot broth or something like that. And a jug of milk. I get very
thirsty.'

'She sweats a lot,' Lili said, holding up the stained cotton dress
Carla had worn earlier.

74

Hugh leaned across and placed his palm on Carla's forehead. She jumped back as if scalded, appalled by his touch. She bit her lip, fighting an urge to rush to the bathroom and scrub the patch of skin raw.

'Sensitive?' he said. 'Do you want me to get you a doctor?'

'I'm okay.' Lili had moved to the doorway. 'One thing,' Carla said. 'The potty needs emptying. Lili, would you mind?'

'I have to go now,' the girl said. 'I will be back Saturday morning.'

When Lili had gone Carla said, 'She's slimy. She gives me the creeps.'

'And me? I give you the creeps too, don't I?'

The question confused her. It was a question she had expected him never to ask, and now that he had asked it she was uncertain of her feelings, uncertain how to answer him.

'I wouldn't say that,' she said without conviction.

'Don't dissemble, Carla. It's good to get these things said once, then forgotten. I want to know why you find my touch repulsive. I'm your father.'

'Last night . . .'

'No, this didn't start last night. Last night was merely the end of my patience, my childish outburst if you like. It isn't only children who suffer frustration—'

'Frustration!' Her voice was teasing. 'Are you frustrated over me, Hugh?'

'All right. Have it your way.'

'Your way's kinkier. Ooh, frustration.' She saw, with satisfaction, that his fists were clenched as he stood up. Go on, hit me with your fist, she thought. Let's see who has more control, shall we? 'Don't fret, papa,' she told him, 'it's supposed to be natural. One of us will grow out of it.'

He was shaking his head, a sad smile on his face. 'All right, Carla. We'll leave it at that. Anything else you want?'

'Letter on the dressing table. Can you post it for me?'

He picked up the letter. 'Who's Marsha Bryce?'

'Oh, didn't I tell you about her? Nice girl. Nympho father-killer. Stabbed her old man through the braces with a carving knife when

75

she was nine, but they let her off with lines. Been on heroin since. You'd like the family too. Lives in this converted brothel incestuously with her five brothers and a queer au pair boy. Lovely ménage.'

'She sounds as if you've got a lot in common. All right, I'll post it.'

'Do they censor letters?'

'That would depend on what you've put in it.'

'I've told her everything that's happened since we got here. I wrote it last night before I . . . went out. But I added some today. So it's right up to date. It's got all my secrets in it, Hugh. Are you going to steam it open first?' She giggled. 'You won't understand it. Don't suppose the censor would either. Marsh will, though. It's in—' She altered her voice to a harsh whisper. '—secret code.'

'You're as healthy as I am,' he said, with sudden realisation. 'You've been play-acting for some reason.'

Carla turned her face to the pillow. 'Thanks,' she said flatly.

'I'm sorry if you're offended. You can't blame me for not knowing how to take you.'

'Take me, Hugh. I'm yours.'

'Shut up.' He strode towards the door.

'I really can't get to the bathroom, you know,' she called. 'Honestly. Could I have a bowl of water for washing? And some soap and a towel. A bath towel, so I can have a strip wash.'

He said, 'I'll send someone up with them.'

'And if I get worse and die don't bother to apologise to me.'

Frau Holzbaum brought her the milk and broth and found her shivering.

Carla kept her eyes closed, sensing the woman's uncertainty. Frau Holzbaum shook her gently. Carla groaned. Then the old woman hurried out.

A few minutes later Hugh was by her bedside.

'Carla,' he said. 'You awake?' She grunted, turning slowly, opening her eyes slowly. 'I'm getting you a doctor,' Hugh said.

'Get me some blankets. I'm cold.'

'Okay, but a doctor.'

'No. See how I am in the morning. Please. If I'm not better then

76

you can. But I will be.' Seeing the hesitation in him she went on: 'I've had this before. At school. It goes away on its own.'

'What is it?'

'They don't know. Bug of some kind. Could I have those blankets?'

Hugh fetched her two grey woollen blankets and a cup of hot cocoa.

'Careful,' he warned, 'it's scalding.'

'Leave it,' Carla said. 'I'll drink it after. Let me sleep.'

Then she closed her eyes and allowed the shivering to subside noticeably.

When Hugh had tiptoed out and closed the door silently behind him, Carla permitted herself a smile.

Ten minutes later she was pulling the wardrobe away from the wall.

First she carried the broth through. Then she went back for the cocoa, stopping to listen at the hall door and at Hugh's door. When she was satisfied that she'd been left to sleep, she dragged the wardrobe to behind her.

He was still on his pile of sacks, where she had left him, under the boarded-over window. He was in the semi-sleep of the starving. Carla tried to sit him up, but even in his undernourished state he was too heavy for her.

'Try and sit up,' she said. 'Setzen Sie sich auf. Food. Essen.' She smacked her lips, as if for a baby and got a weak acknowledgement from him. His eyes were surprisingly bright in the cheesy, emaciated face. She suspected that if his lips weren't so horribly cracked he would be laughing, finding his predicament a huge joke. That was how he had struck her earlier in the day, when she'd first found him there, lying helpless in his own filth in the old meat store. It still smelled of meat, and of him, and she hated the place. It was running with damp, dark and crawly, a little hole of a place not more than eight feet by ten. A steel beam ran along the ceiling from one end of it to the other and, incredibly, it contained a small fireplace. But thank God she hadn't yet seen a rat.

Now she had him taking tiny spoonfuls of the broth, though much of it dribbled back, milky-white like the drool of an infant, down his heavily stubbled chin. The sight of it encouraged Carla to make mothering sounds as she fed him. 'Take some more. Good boy. One more. That's fine.' She remembered having read something once about not overloading a shrunken stomach. Or had it been a television programme about prisoners of war? Anyway, it seemed they usually bolted their first wholesome food and then brought the lot back. 'Enough now,' she told him, 'I'm not having you sick it up over me. You're in enough of a state as it is.' Then something about those eyes made her add: 'Did you understand that? Can you blink? Of course you can blink. Silly cow. Blink if you can understand what I'm saying.'

He blinked three times.

'Fantastic. Don't try and talk or you'll open your lips and they'll bleed. They're all cracked. Understand? Blink once for yes, twice for no.'

He blinked once, to show that he understood. Then a frantic series of blinks followed. His lips started to move. Carla reached out and touched his brittle lips with her finger, surprised that she could bring herself to do it. Yet the odd thing was she didn't find him at all repulsive. His filth was no more unpleasant to her than her own would have been in the same circumstances. Hugh, sterile, talced and lotioned Hugh, was more repulsive to her than this strange, half-starved man she'd found in a disused cold-room. Only the room itself disgusted her.

'No talkee,' she said. 'Listen, in a minute I'm going to get some water and wash you. Then I'm going to wrap you in blankets and you're going to sleep. Okay? We'll have a proper chat in the morning, when my father's gone out.' There was another frantic bout of blinking. She knew intuitively what it signified and said: 'Don't worry. I haven't told him about you. I don't trust him either, or his fancy piece. You're my secret. Okay?' One blink.

She hung her night-light from the steel beam, using the nylon draw-cord from a duffel bag, and washed him in the small circle of light it provided. She wrinkled her nose as she pulled off his clothes—baggy black trousers, a shredded tan-coloured sweater, a frayed shirt

78

black with grime, no undervest, a reeking pair of underpants, holed socks.

'God, how long have you been sleeping rough? Never mind. Look, I'll try and get this lot washed. Meantime you can wrap yourself in these blankets. And you can have my potty. Do you understand "potty"?' He blinked once. 'Good. Or I'd have put you in nappies.'

She smiled at him. When he tried to smile back his lip split and a tiny trickle of blood ran down his chin. She wiped it away with a piece of damp tissue, shaking her head at him.

Then the sight of him wrapped in the blankets made her want to weep. Those dark circles around his eyes, she thought, looking hard at him, they were doing it. There was nothing remarkable about the eyes at all. The dark circles were highlighting them, but the effect was fantastic. And the way his blue-black beard stubble glistened in the torchlight. His dependence excited her, and his trust, his need—what effect did that have? Unanalysable. But good.

Oh, very good.

Her morning was an agony of frustration. Hugh was scheduled to interview a DDR official in the afternoon and spent the morning in his room, typing up notes. She heard him leave the room only once, to go to the bathroom. The rest of the time he was at the typewriter, clearly audible through the wall. Every now and again he would stop, and then Carla would imagine him cocking his head to listen for any sounds she might be making. She would oblige with a scraping-chair sound, a dropping-shoe noise. Once she stationed herself by the connecting door and contrived a silence in response to his pause, even suppressing her breathing. Before long he called through the wall: 'Everything all right in there? Carla?' Carla made no sound. She heard him pull his chair back from the table where he was working and cross the room to the communicating door. She heard him knock and made no sound.

When, after a few moments, he burst in, he found her standing, arms akimbo, facing him.

'Peekaboo,' she said.

Over lunch (her first meal in the dining room for two days) she

79

found herself willing him to fold his napkin in that deliberate, mannered way of his when he was about to leave the table. Instead, he seemed to linger deliberately over the meal. And again he disconcerted her by watching her eat. She spent five minutes dicing a potato into the tiniest possible slivers, then pushed the heap of potato to one side of her plate. She began cutting up cabbage, labelling the pieces, Hugh, Lili, Frau Holzbaum.

'You still haven't got your appetite back, I see.'

'I can't eat when I'm being watched. Can't pee either.'

'Don't be crude, Carla. Are you sure it's gone, your bug?'

'Told you. It's a twenty-four hour thing. Or forty-eight, or some number like that. Can't remember.'

'I'd be happier if you saw a doctor.'

'Communist doctors give everyone the same medicine, whatever they've got,' she said to annoy him.

'Who told you that rubbish?'

She shrugged. 'Well-known fact. Anyway, all I need is building up. I usually take a course of Complan after one of these bugs. Can you get that in the Workers' Paradise?'

'There'll be an equivalent. Meat will help build you up.' He indicated her plate with his knife.

'Their meat's yuchy.' She poked at the piece of ham on her plate.

'I tell you what. If you haven't gone vegetarian I'll take you to the Berolina-Keller tomorrow, in the Alex'platz, and you can have the best steak east of the Pecos.'

'What about the Complan?'

'That too.'

'When?'

'On my way back, this afternoon. Do you think you can hold out that long?'

'Thought I might go out myself and get it.'

'Ah,' Hugh said. 'So that's it. Forget it, Carla. No Wanderlust. Strengst verboten, all right?'

'Can't stop me,' she pouted.

'Let's not start that again. Look, Carla, this city . . . This isn't Haywards Heath. You can't just wander around at will and expect kindly bobbies to give you tea and send for me every time. That's a reality you're just going to have to learn to live with.'

'You've got plans for me, haven't you?'

'What?'

'You've got it all worked out. Where I can go, when I can go. And when I can't. Maybe there's something you didn't bargain for, though.'

'And what might that be?'

'That's my secret.'

Hugh sighed. 'Yes, you're a remarkably secretive girl, Carla.

'Wonder where I get it from.'

'Anyway,' he said, folding the napkin and standing up, 'you're going out tomorrow. You've only this afternoon to get through. Have a read of that Brockhaus I bought you.'

'Big deal. Will I be on a leash? Tomorrow, when you take me walkies.'

Hugh left without answering.

She stood at her window and watched him drive away in the red Volkswagen. Then she forced herself to remain there a further ten minutes in case he doubled back. Only when she was satisfied that he had genuinely gone did she make her way down to the lobby.

Frau Holzbaum was behind the desk.

As Carla approached the main door, walking purposefully, the old woman stepped out to intercept her.

'Hello, Gretchen, old thing,' Carla said to her. 'Woof, woof.'

Frau Holzbaum gripped Carla's arm. The grip was painful, terrifyingly strong. Carla struggled against it. 'Get off,' she said. 'Ich bin hungrig. I was going out to get food. Essen.'

But by degrees the old woman was pulling her towards the swing door behind the reception desk. The kitchen lay behind it, Carla knew. Frau Holzbaum was suddenly the old witch of folk tales again, and she, Carla, was Gretel being dragged into the gingerbread cottage. She found she was shrieking now. 'Let go of me, you stinking old bitch.'

'Kommen Sie,' Frau Holzbaum was saying, pulling her.

Then they were in Bruckner's shop, not in the kitchen at all, and

81

she had lost the power of movement. Herr Bruckner, in a bloody apron, was slicing ham wafer thin with a fat-smeared, long-bladed knife. He looked up, unsmiling, and craned to see who was in the doorway.

'That you, Christa? I want you.'

She felt her lips move but no sound seemed to come out. Frau Holzbaum thrust a thick ham sandwich into her trembling hands and shooed her, grinning, out of the kitchen.

Visiting him in the Secret Annexe had a calming effect on her, as she had known it would. She felt secure there, free of the confusion that troubled her outside. For a while she just sat and listened to his laboured breathing, occasionally reaching out to stroke his cheek soothingly, as if by doing so she was soothing herself. And later, when the sense of her presence awoke him, they shared a silence totally different from the silences she knew with her father. He seemed to know this was a place of peace for her, as much her haven as his, somewhere just to be alive and free of constraint.

Eventually, she said, 'Don't talk unless you feel up to it.' But she moistened his lips with the water she'd brought in the cocoa cup.

When he spoke his voice was hardly more than a hoarse whisper, yet accentless. 'Turn the light away,' he said. 'It's hurting my eyes.'

'I washed your clothes,' she told him. 'In the bath. The water went grey. They're drying in my room.'

'Burn them.'

'I might have to take the blankets back. You'd freeze. You could do with a fire in here.'

'I'm not cold.'

'I am. I think this used to be the cold room. For the shop.' Then, 'How long have you been here?'

He hesitated. He seemed uncertain. 'Few days. What day is it?'

'Friday. The seventh.'

'Few days,' he repeated. 'I took a chance on you. Got in through the shop.'

'Oh.' That was worth knowing. If he'd got in through the shop

82

she could get out the same way if she had to. But she didn't press him. 'Don't talk too much straight away,' she said.

'They're looking for me.' His voice cracked, making him cough. A coughing fit developed which took him over. She fed him a mouthful of water. 'They're looking,' he said again. 'I can't stay here.'

'Why not? Don't you trust me?'

He reached his hand out under the blanket and she took it and squeezed it, knowing he wasn't strong enough to make the gesture. And again she had the sensation of caring for a child. It made her feel protective, absurdly almost ready to give her life for him. It was an uncomfortable, scarcely bearable feeling. She deliberately destroyed the moment by withdrawing her hand.

'We don't even know each other,' Carla said. 'We don't know anything about each other.' He smiled. 'What are you thinking?'

'I was thinking what a brave and unusual person you are, Fräulein, and I was wondering why you should want to help me.'

'Carla,' she said, 'not Fräulein. And that sounds patronising, and you aren't old enough to patronise. You're just a bit haggard.'

'Why do you want to help me?'

'I'm not sure. It's hard to say without sounding all sort of true-blue and goody-goody, but if you hate a system it's no good just saying how rotten it is—even if it's someone else's system and you don't have to live in it. You ought to help do something about it—change it, or if you can't change it, undermine it. I do hate the way people have to live here. I suppose I just want to help someone get away from it, and you happened to turn up. Sort of. I haven't thought it out properly yet. Something like that.'

'I was always sure about you,' he said. 'But I watched you anyway, and then I thought: "I'll take a chance on her. It's not much of a chance, and if I'm wrong I'll be no worse off in the end." What worries me most is what he'd do to you—not to me—if he found out.'

'Who?' Carla said, suddenly out of touch with him.

'You know him better than I do, of course. Better not to think about it. Unless you want to change your mind.'

'About helping you?'

83

'If you could just hide me for a few days, that's all, till I get my strength back . . .'

'Look, I know I'm only a schoolgirl and you're maturer than me. I know all that, but helping you get away would be something so fantastic for me, for *me*, to do for myself . . . See, I want it for selfish reasons, so don't make me out to be all noble and self-sacrificing, because that's not why I want to do it. And if it helps me get back at my father so much the better. That's the honest truth. I've been looking for something like this all my bloody life. I don't care if it's dangerous, I want it to be dangerous because things aren't important otherwise, unless someone else wants to prevent them—God, I'm not making sense to you, but I know what I mean. You'll just have to take my word for it. I don't even care if you turn out to be part of some thrillerish plot they've cooked up against me, my father and that lot, don't care if you're a trap I've walked into because it's what I wanted to do. Do you understand that? I'm committing myself, even if it doesn't make good political sense. Speech over.'

She paused and waited for his reaction, surprised at her own outburst. In the silence that followed she could hear him groping for the water cup. She picked it up and held it for him while he drank.

'I want you to take your time,' he said. 'Don't make up your mind yet.'

'But I've bloodywell made it up,' she shouted, then lowered her voice, repeating, 'I've already made up my mind. That's what I was just telling you.'

'I used to play up here years ago,' he said reminiscently. 'You'd have been a baby, but I wish we'd known each other then. Ever hear anybody mention me? Karl Silbermann.'

'I'm not from here. I'm only staying here.' Why was it so hard to get through to him? 'Tell me how I can help, Karl,' she pleaded. 'Tell me where to go.'

Karl said, 'There's a man in Taubenstrasse who can help.'

Afterwards, when Carla played the scene back in her mind, there were aspects of it that disturbed her, things that didn't make sense. How, if Karl had been several days in a blind store-room, could he

84

have watched her? Why did he ask if she'd heard anyone mention him? And why, when she was talking to him, did she have the uncomfortable feeling that instead of listening to what she said and responding to her words, he was speaking from a script? As if it were impossible for him to deviate from his lines. As if he'd been rehearsed thoroughly but wasn't enough of an actor to carry off the role. Another nagging worry was his speech—the accentless, fluent speech of . . . of what? What did it remind her of, his precise and perfect speech? The wartime recordings of that traitor—what was his name? —Lord Something, Lord Cackle or some such derisive name. A well-schooled spy (and she found it hard enough to believe in the existence of spies at all) would probably speak the kind of English Karl spoke.

The implications were even more disturbing. If spies weren't mythical entities, like mediaeval demons, and if Karl wanted her to deceive her father, what would that make Hugh?

On the side of the angels?

Yet all this was the product of reasoning. It took no account of her non-rational side, that part of her which knew she could trust Karl completely and wanted to trust him, but didn't want to trust her father. He had to be the villain of the piece. Anything else would have been unacceptable. The Secret Annexe made the difference. That was their place, belonged to the young. There were no doubts or arguments in her mind when she sat with Karl in the cold room, no thoughts then of the penalties for helping an East German citizen to escape to the west. Yet, strangely enough, her danger seemed real only then. In her bedroom it wasn't quite believable that she was helping a fugitive and risked imprisonment for it. In Sussex, two hours' flight time away, she'd be doing Social Projects. The Arts Fifth would be learning responsible citizenship by decorating old folks' flats and giving tea parties for deprived children; she, meanwhile, was setting herself against a political system that ordered half the world.

What I Did in My Summer Holidays.

Carla said, 'Hugh, ever thought of writing a spy thriller?'

'No. Why?'

'You'd make more money out of it than *Unknown Cities of the World*. I mean, isn't East Berlin supposed to be the spy capital or something?'

'There are espionage circles in every major city,' Hugh said. 'Yes, I suppose East Berlin has its fair share. Why the sudden interest in my writing?'

'I like spy novels. I suppose I'd like it if you wrote one. You've got all the material here, haven't you?'

'I might mention it in my book. Come on, Carla, what are you driving at? You're much too devious to make small talk. And you don't give a damn what I write.'

'Be like that, then.'

'What is it you want to know?'

'What?'

He was smiling. 'You want to know something about espionage. Right? And instead of asking me directly you go through all this rigmarole about spy novels. So what do you want to know?'

She shrugged. 'Just find it hard to believe they really exist. I don't know. I suppose I expected to see hordes of men in trench coats and those turned-down hats marching around with guns. Taking pot-shots at each other. *Spy Who Came in From the Cold* and all that.'

'Ah. Well, they do exist, but they don't march in regimental formation or wear uniform. You wouldn't know one if you saw one. They don't carry guns normally. Ball pens are a better bet, and not the ones that squirt cyanide or shoot darts. Your typical intelligence agent is more likely to be a clerk in a coding room, or an office cleaner who empties waste baskets, or a shopkeeper who knows someone who empties waste baskets.'

'What about Lili?' Carla said. 'Could she be a spy?'

'Lili's a guide. Her job is to show me what I want to see, and to show it—understandably—in its most favourable light. I suppose if I tried to get too close to things that didn't concern me she might, as a State official, have to steer me away. That hardly makes her a spy.'

'Yours would be a good cover—is that the right word?—for spying, wouldn't it?'

86

'Too obvious. But I'll tell you something, strictly between our two selves. I wouldn't be surprised if Frau Holzbaum were the Hausvertrauensfrau for this place. All the apartment blocks have them, and I should think the hotels do too. If I'm right she'd be a very minor functionary—sort of spare-time job, you know? Her job would be to report to the authorities every month or so on anything unusual or suspicious—sorry, suspect—the tenants did. Guests, in this case. But don't worry about it. Most of the reports they get from Hausvertrauensleute would be ninety percent gossip and consignable to the waste bin, unread.'

'Where the spies could pick it up.'

He laughed. 'Touché. In case you're concerned, she wouldn't be interested in your mysterious tapping, Carla. Heard it since?' She shook her head. 'You haven't been worrying about that, have you? Aha!'

'Sort of,' she said coyly.

'Well, don't any more. Frau Holzbaum wouldn't waste ink on it. She's not a bad old stick, you know.'

'Thanks for telling me, though.'

'I'm only guessing, mind. No,' he said, 'the real thorn in the DDR's side is the Fluchthelfer.' He fished in a pocket for his pipe. 'Those are the professionals who help dissidents escape to West Berlin. Except that more often than not they merely exploit the people they're supposed to be helping, and, much worse, they maintain the tension between east and west in this part of the world. Anyone who helped eradicate the Fluchthelfer would be doing a service to both sides. Still curious?'

'Just asking,' Carla said. 'Saves looking in the Yellow Pages.'

'I'm glad you didn't make it another of your little secrets. It's childish to keep secrets, Carla.'

They spent most of Saturday morning in HO-Warenhaus, the largest state-owned store in East Berlin. Outside, in Alexanderplatz, a hot, bright day had brought out the people; the fresh sweat of their undeodorised bodies mixing with the smells of sun-warmed concrete and exhaust fumes. Carla had found the mixture intoxicating after her days of confinement in the hotel's gloom. She stared into the brightness of the square, into the windows of its high, new buildings until they blinded her; opened herself like a flower.

Inside, she became drunk with another kind of life: the noisy getting-and-spending swarm of Saturday in the store. The icing. Lili, transformed, girlish, was at the icing too; she licked it straight from the bowl with the insatiable greed of the deprived child.

'But that is almost a week's industrial earnings,' she protested, both awed and disgusted, when Hugh bought Carla a flimsy nightdress: a plain, wishy-washy pink garment of man-made fibre.

'It's doing your economy good,' Hugh said, and bought Carla a case shaped like a cat's head to keep it in. The cat unzipped behind its ears. Carla bought a Russian-made wind-proof cigarette lighter in dull steel, had it gift wrapped and slipped it quickly into her handbag. When Hugh wanted to know what she'd bought Carla told him, coyly 'Don't be nosey. Those who ask don't get.'

'Lili,' Hugh said, 'buy something.'

'But she already has the nightdress,' the girl said. 'And that silly cat.'

'Buy something for yourself.'

Carla said 'Mary Quant's coming in big this year, Lili. The mini's in with the Chelsea set.'

'Yes, we know about miniskirts. But it's all so expensive.'

'I'm paying,' Hugh said.

'Don't be so bourgeois,' Carla urged. The girl's eyes were gleaming, she noticed. That was odd. Lili drove a Wartburg, priced, she seemed to remember, at over 20,000 marks in the Unter den Linden showroom. She made a quick mental calculation. What was that, four years' salary? And although Lili dressed badly, frumpishly, her clothes couldn't be all that cheap. So why all the fuss about buying herself a dress for three or four hundred marks? Nor could it be simple meanness, not if Hugh was paying.

'It isn't bourgeois,' the girl said. 'To buy such things is bourgeois. It is to affront the pride of the industrial labourer.'

'Have this one on capitalism. No arguments, Lili. Carla, help her choose something to wear. A suit, or a dress or something.'

'No, really, I cannot . . .' Lili began, but Carla led her away.

The choice was severely limited: a few racks of high-priced dresses, suits, summer coats; even fewer at astronomical prices, though here there was more variation in cut and quality. Lili rummaged, with nervous haste, through the cheaper dresses.

'There are so many,' she said. 'How can I choose?'

'What about this one?' Carla had pulled a bright red dress in imitation silk from the most expensive rack. The dress was printed with huge blue-and-white flowers.

'No, no,' Lili said.

'What's wrong with it? This is haute couture on Southend beach.'

'Yes, but the price.' She turned over the ticket and gasped. 'No, no.'

'Hugh's got pots of money.'

'Yes, but—'

'He's going to make pots out of this book, Lili. You're helping him, aren't you?'

'But I am paid for that. My job—'

'Balls.'

'Bitte?'

'He wants you to look nice. He's got terribly expensive tastes. You'll only offend him if you get some cheap bit of rag.'

Lili was wavering. She felt the dress, rubbing its fabric between her fingers.

'Where is Southend?'

'Very chic coastal resort in Essex,' Carla said, biting her lip. 'Have you heard of Ascot?'

89

'Ah, yes, the hats.'

'Southend's the same for dresses. Like the feel of it? Genuine imitation silk, that.'

'You don't think it's too . . .'

'Gaudy? Height of fashion, gaudiness. All the rage.'

Lili wanted to wear the dress straight away, but Carla persuaded her to keep it a surprise and it was put in a bag.

They wandered around the departments. Carla bought large quantities of chocolate ('Vitamins,' she explained, 'to build me up.') and tried inching her way towards a cigarette stand. Hugh cut her off.

'You'll get lost,' he said, leading her away.

They ate in the Berolina-Keller. Carla declined steak and settled for goulash because the others were having goulash. She was permitted an inch of thick Hungarian wine, topped up with water.

'Afraid I'll get drunk?'

'Terrified,' Hugh said.

'I get indiscreet when I'm drunk.'

'For Hungarian food,' Lili observed, taking a sip of wine, 'Haus Budapest is better.'

'Is that the one in Kurfürstendamm?'

Hugh threw her a puzzled glance. 'Kurfürstendamm's in West Berlin.'

'Ever been to West Berlin, Lili?' Carla asked.

'Yes. But Haus Budapest is in Karl-Marx-Allee, here in the DDR.'

Carla said, 'What's the one I'm thinking of, then? Something Keller that is.'

'I don't know the restaurants over there.'

'Nor does she,' Hugh said. 'That place we ate in Tuesday night was called Aben.'

'We must have passed it further along. Something Keller.'

'Kurfürstenkeller?'

'Suppose so.'

'What about it?'

'Nothing. Just joining in this sophisticated conversation about restaurants, wasn't I?'

90

Carla deftly tucked her meat under the galushka as Hugh bent over his plate to load his fork. Cleverguts, she thought. And it bloody wasn't Kurfürstenkeller either.

She tuned out their conversation, letting it become a meaningless background drone to her thoughts. A beam of sunlight caught her interest. She began following the progress of dust motes in it with single-minded fascination. Marsha's image sprang into her head, Marsha eating pie and chips in the school refectory. Why hadn't Marsh written to her? Or was it that she seemed as remote, as other-worldly to Marsha as Marsha did to her? She wondered what the effect of her letter would be, with its feverish, hysterical account of secret places behind a bedroom wall and its fantasies of espionage, conspiracy, Machiavellian intrigue. Carla wasn't even sure Marsha would be able to read between the lines sufficiently well to under-stand what she meant, though her dislike of Lili and Hugh and her suspicions of the sinister Frau Holzbaum had been written *en clair*. It seemed so much tripe now she reflected on it in the security and brightness of a crowded restaurant in broad daylight. Lili was just a fatuous, gullible, brainwashed moron. Frau Holzbaum, poor cow, was a simple-minded old busybody, probably in drag. Recalling the tone of her letter, Carla smiled to herself, an adult reflecting on the imaginative excesses of a child. But then, Karl . . .

'. . . do you, Carla?' Hugh was asking.

'Sorry. Do I what?'

'Have a boyfriend.'

'I was just curious,' Lili said.

'What if I have?'

'Carla, you're being rude,' Hugh admonished.

'No,' the guide said, 'if she thinks it is too personal a question . . .'

'All right, I have.'

'How nice for you. Where does he live, your boy?'

'In my cupboard.'

'What a cosy place,' Lili said dryly.

'Yes, he's my bank manager actually.'

'How capitalistic of you.'

'I keep him as a pet. He gets fed on chocolate and left-overs. Okay?'

'Full of vitamins,' Lili said, raising her eyebrows. 'And do you love this pet of yours?'

'I had a pet ant once. Kept it in a matchbox. But I had a crush on it and it died.'

After an awkward pause Lili said, 'Yes, that is the pity of keeping pets. They sometimes die.'

A waiter brought coffee to their table. Hugh changed the subject of conversation to shortages in the DDR.

'That is mostly propaganda by the western press,' the guide said. 'Some fruits, for example, are freely available.'

'Butter's rationed, though, isn't it?' Hugh asked.

'For the sake of the economy. The health of the economy comes before love of luxury in any sensible society.'

'Can I quote you?' he said playfully.

'You are free to do so.'

'Guns before butter,' Carla said, 'like the good old days.'

She had the feeling they were frog-marching her. They penned her in, never letting her stray more than a few feet before cutting in front of her, like a pair of sheepdogs, guiding her back on the path she must walk. They walked briskly south from Alexanderplatz, away from the busy square where she might too easily lose herself, and after taking in the city courthouse in Littenstrasse the three of them, prisoner-and-escort, crossed the Mühlendamm Bridge.

They went via the fish market then, along Breitestrasse towards the library, Carla's mood worsening with constriction and as her feet tired on the hot pavements of the Altstadt. Here, Lili explained, was where Berlin was founded in the thirteenth century; and Carla, all innocence, wanted to know if that meant East Berlin's television tower was the oldest in the world.

As they re-crossed the Spree by the Rathausbrücke Carla glanced across the road and saw two black American soldiers passing on the other side of the bridge. She was startled by them. The taller man seemed to be illustrating a story. He was holding both his arms, robotlike, in front of him as he walked, balancing one fist against the other as if weighing them, or miming car-driving. It was obviously a funny story because the other soldier, a sergeant, was laughing noisily. They came abreast of Carla, separated from her by the width of the roadway, and she heard the sergeant say, 'Not that time it didn't,' which made the other black laugh. Their black skin and silver insignia gleamed momentarily as the sun caught them, then the soldiers rounded a corner.

As they did so it struck her like a shock to the brain that these men belonged to the other world, to Marsha's, to her own world. They came from outside, visiting beyond the wall, and were free to return there. The realisation overwhelmed her, brought her close to panic. Her freedom was illusory. She was a cage-bird released for a while in a room, a prisoner enjoying the freedom of the exercise yard. She wanted to run, again that primal urge to run, to catch the Americans, to throw herself at their feet and beg to be taken away.

The scene unfolded in her mind, a silent film, a melodrama. Herself weeping, pointing accusingly at her captors, at Hugh–Lili, clasping her hands pleadingly to her breast and moving jerkily, her lips thick with rouge; while the Americans threw up their hands in horror and shook their fists angrily at the villainous Hugh. *Rape*! she'd be mouthing. *Abduction*! *The swine*!

In an idle corner of her brain a connection was made. The flimsy pink nightie Hugh had bought her in HO-Warenhaus. That was odd, now she came to think of it. His choice ought to have been more prudish. Perhaps some opaque, ankle-length thing with a choker neck and long sleeves. In red flannel. And when in the shop she'd said, 'Bit daring for you, isn't it?' he'd laughed and answered, 'But it isn't for me, it's for you.' So now she saw herself exhibiting the nightie, pulling it out of its bag there on the bridge, evidence that she was Lolita to Hugh's Humbert. Enter Hugh, calm, controlled, oozing villainous charm and Englishness. *Alas, my daughter has been ill. She is not herself*, with a triumphant leer to the hissing audience. Apologetic, cap-doffing flourishes from the duped Americans, then, and Hugh leads the protesting girl back across the bridge. *Remember what the doctor said about too much sun, my dear.*

'They're from the base in West Berlin,' Hugh was saying.
Lili said, 'They come here to breathe a little free air.'

Carla lost Hugh and Lili in the U-Bahn. A train ride had been Carla's suggestion, and she got her way by pouting and saying 'No-one ever lets me decide anything. I'm not the dog, you know.'

Once on the platform at Alexanderplatz she used a technique similar to one she'd seen in countless films where people gave other people the slip. It involved hanging back some way behind Hugh and Lili as the short subway train clattered in with a rush of warm, electric-scented wind; then delaying (she feigned trouble with her heel) while the train filled up. As the doors were about to close she seemed likely to make it in good time, so Hugh boarded, Lili following. At the last second Carla balked. She tried to make it look as if she was afraid of getting crushed between the doors. Hugh had no time to step back to the platform before the doors closed, and Carla was left behind. It worked, even though she did it badly. She felt clumsy and obvious, and strangely guilty as the train whined out of the station, Hugh frantically signalling to her through the glass. Carla shrugged to convey her helplessness and smiled a brief apology. She was left facing a red-lettered wall poster condemning imperialistic Zionist aggression against the peaceloving Arab states.

It was six stops from Alexanderplatz to Thälmannplatz. The train was a boneshaker, a smelly, rattling old thing with wooden benches polished lustrous by the shifting and sliding of innumerable German rumps. Carla slid about on the seat, nauseated by the train's constant rocking, her nerves punished by its electric whine.

Between Stadtmitte and the Thälmannplatz terminus the train suddenly slowed down. Then it emerged from the tunnel into the half light of a derelict station. She saw a platform patrolled by green-uniformed guards, one at either end, machine pistols slung casually—like cameras—across their shoulders. The train's wheels had taken on a new, slow rhythm, the rhythm of a slow march. The lights dimmed, then brightened again. But the train didn't stop. Once through the guarded subterranean zone it picked up speed and shortly afterwards entered the brightness of Thälmannplatz station. Some of the passengers, she'd noticed, had seemed hypnotised by the experience, staring expressionlessly through the train's windows at the silent platform. Now she sensed the release of their tension as they left the train and hurried up to the open air. Carla checked the map on the subway wall. Just outside Stadtmitte the line ran under Friedrich-strasse north of Checkpoint Charlie; and at that point it was inter-sected by a loop of U-Bahn belonging to the West Berlin system. Once the station had been part of an integrated Berlin underground railway, probably one of its busiest sections. Since the wall had been built neither system used the station, though the West Berlin trains still ran between Kochstrasse and Friedrichstrasse, itself a frontier station. What she had passed through was an underground Death Strip, watched over night and day by border guards.

Somewhat shaken, she came up into Thälmannplatz, a green square overlooking the grassy tumulus of Hitler's bunker and the former site of his chancellery. Beyond that lay West Berlin's Tier-garten. There was an illusion of space here, where on either side of Wilhelmstrasse had been the ministries and embassies of the Third Reich. Now the street was called Otto-Grotewohl-strasse and there were new ministry buildings in it. The rubble had been cleared away, the bunker fenced off. She might have been standing in London's Park Lane.

The sky had clouded over since Carla had left Alexanderplatz, and a chilling wind was blowing. She turned back into the greyness of the city to find Arnold Kreismann.

The streets here, close to the frontier, were empty and echoing. Abandonment hung in the air like dust. Hearing nothing except her own footfall on the cracked stone paving, Carla passed row after row of blank-walled high buildings, some tenements, some with the look of warehouses. She was reminded of a dockland area, for many of the streets ended in fences: as if wharves lay beyond them. Or marshalling yards. Occasionally she had the feeling that she'd in-advertently wandered into a restricted zone, somehow missed one of the warning signs and entered the Death Strip; but that was ir-rational—where the Wall began there was always a fence, always a warning, often a guard patrolling or watching from his tower. The address Karl had given her was in Taubenstrasse, between Mauer-strasse and Friedrichstrasse. He hadn't been certain of the number, but the house was impossible to miss, he'd assured her—somewhere in the fifties, with a brown door and window frames, close to the corner of Kanonierstrasse. Kreismann's name might even be under the knocker. She passed several unnumbered doors on her way along Taubenstrasse and once had to go back a few yards to keep her count. Then she found herself at the corner of Glinkastrasse, but that was the wrong intersection. Karl hadn't mentioned Glinkastrasse. Besides, the numbering was out and none of these houses fitted his description. On most of them the paint had flaked so badly that it was impossible to tell what colour the woodwork had been originally. She walked on and came into Friedrichstrasse. Now that was ridiculous. Karl had been specific about one thing: she was to approach from the Mauer-strasse end to save herself a walk along Friedrichstrasse, where there was more chance of her running into trouble. That meant Kreis-mann's house had to be behind her, the way she'd come. She began to retrace her steps, checking each Gothic-lettered street sign she passed to verify that she was still in Taubenstrasse. She was. But there was no sign saying Kanonierstrasse, and the numbering was still wrong.

She was now back at Glinkastrasse again. She ventured a short way along the intersecting street, hesitated, returned to the crossroads. Her obvious move, of course, would be to knock on one of the doors—any door—and ask where Arnold Kreismann lived. If she tried enough houses eventually she was bound to find somebody who knew the man. The obvious drawback there was that it would be a dangerous thing to do. Dangerous for her, for Karl, for Kreis-mann. The dark sub-world into which she had strayed required a different mode of thinking. There were the Hausvertrauensleute to be considered too. An English girl asking for someone who might be known to the police would rate a red-lettered mention in the monthly report. Why hadn't Karl prepared her better? He should have given her clearer instructions, and a what-did-you-call-those plans? A contingency plan. Instead he'd concentrated on the documents she was to ask Kreismann for—identity card, ration card, labour card, passport. Great, but first find your forger. Anyway, what did he want with all those papers if he was going to tunnel under the Wall or be smuggled through a checkpoint in the boot of a car? Hugh's comment on the Fluchthelfer nagged at her. This Kreismann character was obviously a Fluchthelfer. Yet what worried her most was not the possibility that Kreismann would deceive and exploit Karl, but the fear that Karl for some reason, in some way, might be deceiving her.

She caught herself. She was doing it again. Running from shadows. Fleeing from her mind's phantasmagoria. Grow up, Carla. This is no place for children. The next house, she promised herself. She'd ask at the next house.

As she wandered back and forth along the grey, ruined streets, desperation grew within her, and with it self-loathing. She was a spineless, pathetic little mouse, a stupid, unworthy, unworldly baby who wasn't fit to be trusted with . . . with a letter to post. And a man was trusting her with his life. Well, with his freedom, anyway.

She forced herself to be decisive. She'd knock at the next door she came to. It was a safe decision: this stretch of street ended with a blank wall.

She was alone. All right, she'd ask the first person she saw to help her. Her German wouldn't be up to the task of finding Arnold Kreismann unaided, so she'd ask the first person she came across. At a window, in the street: the first person she saw.

He was a fresh-faced young man in a long leather coat cut in military style. Carla almost laughed aloud at the way she immediately labelled him Stasi—Staatssicherheitsdienst—though it wasn't the stereotype that was funny: it was the ludicrousness of secret policemen wearing what amounted to a uniform, the leather trench coat. But this was a fancy. Leather coats were ubiquitous in East Berlin, and she'd seen enough of them to know it. She approached the man.

He turned out not to live in the Mitte district, but insisted on helping her to find Kreismann. For twenty minutes he knocked on doors in Taubenstrasse and the neighbouring streets, asking whoever answered whether they knew where Arnold Kreismann lived or whether they knew anyone who might know where Kreismann lived. Though his German was rapid Carla was able to follow it most of the time, and the answers were easy to understand, since they were usually accompanied by a shake of the head. One woman had known a Kreisler once, but he had been a shoe manufacturer from Leipzig.

Carla's helper seemed to take the disappointment personally, as if the failure to find Kreismann was his responsibility. Each time there was a negative response to one of his calls he made her abject apologies and promised success next time. She began to worry about this. His manners were disturbing, too. She'd formed the impression that East Germans were blunt, even at their friendliest, like Yorkshiremen. Yet he kept calling her 'gnädiges Fräulein'—a phrase which made her think of Viennese ballrooms under the Habsburgs—and found excuses to touch her all the time. He would support her elbow while they crossed an empty road, clasp her shoulder reassuringly while he promised that however long it took he wouldn't let her search for Kreismann alone. Thank you, she told him, but really she had to go home. Her father would be wondering where she was. When she tried to edge away he caught her sleeve, insisting that Kreismann would most likely be living on the south side of Taubenstrasse. Why? she said. Because we haven't found him on the north side, he answered. And that was when she knew he was a psychopath and panicked. She jerked free of his grip and began running through the deserted streets, not caring which direction she ran in, praying she wouldn't come up against a wall or a fence blocking one of the streets. Behind her she heard him following, calling.

She ran into Friedrichstrasse. A middle aged man and woman were walking on the other side of the road. Without checking for traffic Carla ran across to them. They looked at her, puzzled. Only then did she find the courage to look back, her breath burning in her throat. He was crossing Friedrichstrasse at a fast walk, and he was holding something out to her. The couple had stopped now and were watching. Her hysteria suddenly gone, Carla saw them smile as she took the handbag from him, saw them nod with approval as the man made a slight bow and said, 'Ihre Handtasche, gnädiges Fräulein,' saw them frown when she took the bag without a word, turn and begin to walk away.

It was past five o'clock. It seemed urgent to hurry back. She crossed Unter den Linden against the lights and drew angry, high-pitched toots from the horns of several cars. A lorry had to slow for her and the driver shouted something, though Carla didn't hear what he shouted. She was thinking about the man in the leather coat, wondering how much of his menace she had imagined. And if he was not the charming, old-world innocent the couple obviously thought him, what was he? And was there a connection with Kreismann? Or was it pure chance that on a lonely street in broad daylight she'd met a headcase who'd insisted on helping her find Arnold Kreismann? But she hadn't found Kreismann. Nobody had heard of him. Not in Taubenstrasse, not in Glinkastrasse, not in Mauerstrasse. She preferred not to think, for the moment, about the implications of that.

Carla passed under the railway bridge and turned into Friedrichstrasse station. Here was the crossing point for West Berliners, and here, too, foreigners could leave the DDR. If they had the right papers. The S-Bahn crossed the Wall on an elevated section, and Lehrter Stadtbahnhof was five minutes away. She thought of the two American soldiers on the bridge. Her earlier despair had been replaced by sadness, as if she was beginning to accept that she would never get out of East Berlin. And how did you tell the difference between fantasy and premonition?

Before taking the train back to Prenzlauerberg she bought two hundred Casinos at a tobacco kiosk. She smoked one straight away, lighting it with her new Russian lighter. It was harsh and bitter-tasting, and she threw it on the tracks half consumed.

Lili had gone by the time Carla reached the hotel. She had to face Hugh alone. He swept into her room, making her cringe, and she thought he was going to strike her again. The small part of her mind that wasn't inactive with terror wondered at his anger. It seemed disproportionate, excessive; she was reminded of a bad actor hamming extreme rage, a village hall King Lear.

He thundered at her, shaking his finger in her face. 'Where the hell have you been?' And afraid as she was, she wanted to laugh.

'I waited for you. On the platform.'

99

'You bloody little liar. We came back on the next train. You weren't there.'

'You weren't on the next train,' she bluffed. The coolness of her own reply surprised her, yet she could feel her legs wobbling under her.

'We took the next train back,' he said, slightly less sure of himself.

Carla shook her head. 'Then there must have been one in between. When you weren't on it I thought you thought I'd go back to the hotel, so I didn't wait any more.'

'And it took you two hours to get back here?'

'I got on the wrong train.'

'That nonsense with your shoe,' he said, 'you did that deliberately. My God, you're a cunning little animal. I want to know where you were in the last two hours.'

His voice was more controlled now. Her confidence growing, Carla sat on the bed and kicked off her shoes. Then she lay back and clasped her hands behind her head.

'Where do you think I was?'

He was at the bed in three strides, looming over her, his hand raised.

'That's the last time you'll use that tone to me.'

Carla said, 'If you touch me I'll scream this bloody hotel down.'

He lowered his hand. 'I have no intention of touching you.' After a long pause he said, 'I'm giving up on you, Carla. Lili's right about you, you're ineducable.'

'Does that mean I can do what I like?'

'It means you'll get no more warnings from me,' he said.

'Am I under close arrest or something?'

Hugh left without answering.

Another of the night tasks—lighting Karl's fire—was her biggest problem. The problem was fuel. She had the Russian cigarette lighter, and she stole paper for kindling from the hotel dustbins, stuffing them under her clothing for the nerve-stretching journey back to her room. But none of the other rubbish she found there would burn well. She experimented with coffee grounds, tea leaves and potato peelings, laying them in the sun on her window sill (the window closed against the smell) to dry; but without a base of more combustible fuel they merely smouldered and made conspicuous amounts of smoke. Then, on the Monday following her search for Kreismann, she found two wooden crates in the yard where the dustbins were kept.

The yard must have been shared by the butcher's shop next door, because the crates were marked: Bruckner, Berlin: Kalbleber, 20 Büchsen. The crates were splotched with brown and yellow stains on the inside and around their edges, so Bruckner must have used them for some other purpose than their original one as a container for tinned calf's liver. Perhaps he'd kept offal in them. Being dry, they burned well, giving off a smell Carla wrinkled her nose at but which Karl said was appetising. Well, he was the starving one. The crates lasted four nights, but by the time they were gone Karl had recovered enough not to need a fire, though the room remained cold and damp. Carla was relieved because the improvement in Karl meant, among other things, that she no longer had to forage for fuel. The trip she'd made with Bruckner's crates had given her some bad moments, moments when her carefully prepared cover story fell apart in her head, too fragile to be brought out. The story—in case she met any-one on the stairs—was that she was bored and wanted to try her hand at model-making; she'd looked up the German for it, determined to brazen out any such encounter, even to the point of asking for glue and a fretsaw. But she hadn't met anybody on the stairs, and Herr Bruckner would no doubt assume the hotel had expropriated his crates. He could sort that out with Frau Holzbaum.

She made rugs and she made candles. The candles were a stop-gap until she could get out again to buy some. They were a flop. Carla made them by collecting congealed bacon grease and pork fat from an after-dinner litter in the dining room and forming a blob of it around a length of string. She made two of these fatty candles, seating them in thick-bottomed drinking glasses (taken from the same source as the fat). They burned well enough and gave a fairly constant, if dim, light. They were unsuccessful for different reasons. Carla couldn't stand the smell of them and vomited copiously into the chamber pot. Karl reacted violently to the sight of them and broke one of the glasses with a kick. He said they reminded him of death and refused to have them in the cold room with him, preferring darkness.

The rugs she fashioned from the piece of hemp matting which protected the underside of her mattress from the naked bed springs. Cutting it in half, she made a rug from each half and used sacks for underlay. The rugs gave the place an arty-crafty look that Carla found pleasing: a contemporary touch, a woman's touch.

She made other practical provisions. She stuck four pencils under the wardrobe as rollers, one under each corner, and fixed a loop of string to its back so that she could pull it easily and silently to behind her. Her hope was that if anyone came into her bedroom while she was with Karl, it would look as if she'd popped out to the bathroom.

They were at a loss how best to use the steel rail that ran from end to end of the cold room about a foot below the ceiling. Four heavy-gauge double hooks hung from it, presumably supports for sides of beef or bacon that Herr Bruckner had suspended there in the days when the room had been used to store meat. Carla finally hung two of her brightest dresses from them, side by side, as a makeshift tapestry-cum-room-divider. They gave the cosy illusion of two tiny cubicles and made the place seem less forbidding, imposed a comforting architectural control on its austerity.

Hugh was normally out all day. Mealtimes, when Carla saw him, were silent, strained affairs, unless she was in a Hugh-baiting mood. Then she would work at making him lose his temper in public, scoring herself for each degree of anger she roused in him. Once she got an eight (ten was reserved for crockery-smashing with some foaming at the mouth) by showing him the number she had written on her arm in ball-pen ink. He had stalked out of the dining room, leaving his ersatz coffee untouched. But that same evening, at dinner, his mood was conciliatory.

'I forgot,' he said, 'that people of your generation can't appreciate the full significance of that. I'm sorry, Carla.'

'At least they got Red Cross parcels,' she retorted.

'I thought you already had your year's supply of chocolate and cigarettes. Besides,' he added, 'your incarceration's self-imposed. If you want to come with Lili and me all you have to do is agree to act like a responsible human being.'

'Oh, to see the sky again, to touch the good earth again. To feel the fresh wind on one's face . . .'

'You've got the yard, haven't you?'

'It stinks, and so does Frau Holzbaum. Anyway, I've started a tunnel. It begins under my bed and runs to West Berlin.' She raised her water glass. 'Here's to next Christmas in Blighty, chaps.'

'Is that why you're starving yourself? To authenticate your fantasy? Perhaps you'd like me to whip you or beat you over the head with a rifle butt.'

'Ooh. You know how to please a girl, Hugh. Had experience, have you?'

'Only on the receiving end,' he said quietly.

But when Carla tried to pump him he changed the subject. The hint intrigued her. She made an effort to recall what he'd told her in the past about his war, but found nothing definite in her memory. Yet she felt there was a contradiction somewhere and it worried her. What was it? It was more than just the unlikely image of Hugh suffering, which she found impossible to imagine. It had to do with something she thought she knew about his war, something he'd told her long ago about having been there at the end, fighting in the last days of the war. She probed for the memory, which lay just below the conscious level, tantalisingly close but too slippery to grasp and hold. Yes, he'd told her about it years before, so many years that he thought she wouldn't remember. But she did remember.

She smiled across at him and saw a puzzled look pass across his face as he stuffed meat into it.

The war ended in Berlin, didn't it? Ah, that was it. He must have shown her a photograph because it came to her now as a black-and-white visual memory. Blackened ruins half obscured by smoke and streets piled with rubble, and the picture showed him marching in a ragged column of old men and boys with a rifle on his shoulder. Unshaven. Collarless. Strange.

Broader about the chest.

Brutish in appearance.

Older.

She frowned at the unwelcome image.

Whoever it was, it wasn't Hugh.

She kept up her complaints more to serve appearances than because she resented being confined. There were two Berlins; the dull, soul-eroding Berlin of the first days; and the Berlin which included Karl and therefore needed no other diversions. This was the city she now inhabited. So she welcomed being left at the hotel all day and most evenings, and, embracing the punishment, took every opportunity to compound the offence. When Lili turned up on the Tuesday evening wearing her new dress (they were going to a reception), Carla threw an hysterical laughing fit. She rolled helplessly on the floor and pointed at Lili, going into renewed fits at the sight of her dressed for Southend beach. Without a word—Hugh's face had been confirmation enough—the girl had turned and gone home to change. For two days afterwards Lili had avoided the hotel, picking Hugh up in her car on the corner of the street and delivering him back to the same place. Carla had been exultant. The danger of reprieve removed, she was free to cocoon herself in the little space behind the wall, safe in its darkness, until Hugh returned her to England.

The cold room had come to seem a normal environment. Familiarity had done that. She was even developing night-sight, like Karl, and the darkness no longer frightened her. She found it acceptable to sit there for hours on end with him, like two rabbits in a burrow, while the predators scoured the daylight world. She preferred it, though, when they didn't talk. In the silence it was easier to be sure of him, without misgivings. Only when they spoke did she sometimes feel intrusive. It embarrassed her when Karl's speech was disjointed, as it often was, and then her feeling would be that she'd eavesdropped on his spoken thoughts or that he was slightly delirious and rambling.

At those times it helped to touch him, to feel his forehead (thankfully always cool), to hold his hand like a confessor encouraging him to shed the last of his inhibitions. But after the last there was always another, always a distance between them—however much it narrowed—that refused to close entirely. It was a lesion that healed without knitting together, and her fear was that it might fester.

Karl had surprised her by taking the news about Kreismann philosophically.

'He was a good man. More important, he was trustworthy.'

'Well,' Carla said, 'where is he, then? Why wasn't he there when you needed him?'

He muttered something. When she asked him what he'd said he refused to repeat it. This annoyed her. 'We might have found him,' she said, 'if you'd given proper directions.' She'd checked in Hugh's Baedeker, comparing it with her own. Glinkastrasse, it turned out, was Kanonierstrasse. It had been re-named. Lili said it happened all the time. Carla had heard her tell Hugh that she often got confused herself, and she was a guide. But it didn't excuse Karl. If something was really important you went to any lengths to get it right, and she'd told him so. He hadn't answered.

Now he said, ' "We"?'

So she told him about the man in the leather coat and for the first time saw him agitated. His tone was urgent as he asked her to describe the man's manner. She shrugged, which made him angry. Had the man asked any questions about Kreismann? About her? Had he followed her?

'I thought he was following me,' she admitted, 'but he only wanted to give me my handbag back. I must have dropped it.'

'Do you remember dropping it?'

'No, but I must have, mustn't I?'

'What was in it?'

'What, in the bag? Usual sort of thing. I don't know. Comb, brush, hankie. He didn't pinch anything, if that's what you're getting at.'

'What about your papers? Were your papers in the bag?'

'What papers? I don't have any papers.'

'He'll know who you are now,' Karl said peevishly. 'And where you live. Do you think it matters that he didn't follow you home? He knows.'

'I don't get it,' she said.

'Sweet God, and you actually asked him to help you find Arnold.'

'And if your bloody directions had been any good,' she defended, 'I'd have found him on my own. Assuming he exists.'

'He probably doesn't any more. I suppose you know it's only a matter of time now before they pick me up.'

She didn't like him in that mood. But in the days that followed his despondency lifted as Carla was able to assure him that nobody was keeping watch on the building.

She would check the street from her window several times a day, looking, as Karl had instructed her, for the usual rather than the un-usual. These, he said, were the signs of police surveillance: not a man with an upturned collar standing under a lamppost reading yester-day's newspaper, or a black Mercedes parked day and night on the same spot; but someone working by a desk at the window opposite, or a team of workmen digging up the drains. If anything, though, Carla noticed fewer people in the street below than she had seen the week before, and even less traffic. Hugh and Lili no longer parked their cars below her window. Lili must be leaving her car in another part of the street beyond Carla's range of vision, and Hugh, presum-ably, had found somewhere to garage his.

Frau Holzbaum shocked her one evening with an invitation to watch television in her living room. The hotel's tiny guest lounge had no such facilities, not even a radio. It contained a few worn armchairs and a small pedestal table loaded with back numbers of *Neues Deutschland* and some news magazines. The place reminded Carla of a dentist's waiting room. She'd sat in it once for ten minutes, hoping that one of the hotel's elusive guests (she'd seen three in the dining room, all old, all sullen) might come in. Nobody did, and the papers were verbose and dull. Ninety percent propaganda, ten percent news, all of it boring. Unreadable.

She went out of curiosity, apprehension tickling her nerves. But

the gingerbread cottage proved to be ordinary enough. Frau Holzbaum's living quarters smelled of cabbage and of Frau Holzbaum.
The room they sat in was heavily overfurnished and looked like the
back room of an antique shop. There was a vast dresser with curlicues,
an assortment of plain wooden chairs, two lumpy armchairs covered
with powdery brown leather, a pair of occasional tables with scal-
loped edges, and several unidentifiable pieces. One, she thought, was
a commode. Her impression was of unrelieved brownness. Even the
wedding photograph on the dresser was brown, or was that what
they called sepia? Herr and Frau Holzbaum, young, stiff, unsmiling.
When would it have been taken? Some time in the late 'twenties,
Carla guessed. Herr H was wearing a celluloid collar, the palest of
browns, and the light oak face of his bride had a certain severe beauty.
It reminded her of someone, but she couldn't think who.

She perched uncomfortably on the edge of one of the hard chairs
and looked at the television, a robust square box dark brown and
glossy with polish, a doily on top of it protecting it from nothing.

They watched an educational programme called *English for You*.
Lesson Twelve was entitled 'Going Shopping'. Carla hoped for
nostalgic exteriors of an English street, but all the shots were phoney
interiors and the emphasis was on British weights and measures rather
than authenticity. The old woman made notes on a pad, looking up
once to say, 'Pound is money.'

'And weight.'

'I wish now to purchase a dozen eggs,' came from the television.
'But fresh eggs, please. New-laid eggs.' Frau Holzbaum made another
note, her mouth moving silently.

'Is your English good?' Carla asked uneasily, her mind flying back
over what she'd said in the old woman's hearing.

'It becomes.' And as if she thought it a fine idiomatic phrase
repeated, 'It becomes.'

'Moonlight becomes you,' Carla said.

'Yes,' Frau Holzbaum answered. 'Since one year am I learning.'

'. . . and a joint of sirloin,' the shopper was saying.

Frau Holzbaum looked appealingly at Carla. Yes, Carla was thinking, I bet you don't see much of that these days, Gretchen, old girl.

And translated, 'Und ein Lendenbraten', which brought a smile from Frau Holzbaum.

Then there was a tour of a rubber factory, followed by a news report —production figures, sports results, a visit by a Russian diplomat— and finally a Czech film about a lost child. Frau Holzbaum made her tea while she watched it. Carla drank it left-handed and became absorbed in the film, knowing the little boy would be found because this was a fiction, but fearing for him, fearing for his life, intent as a child herself on the flickering black-and-white images of his wanderings. Yet when the film ended with the boy in his father's arms, she felt a tremendous sadness, as if she'd been cheated of the truth.

Her eyes were streaming, and that was absurd as well as embarrassing, because she was no sentimentalist. She looked helplessly across at Frau Holzbaum, but the old woman had fallen asleep in her chair. Her mouth hung open. Soon she'd begin to snore.

For a moment Carla was tempted to twiddle the knobs on the set in the hope of finding a West German station, something marvellously frivolous like the Eurovision Song Contest or Jeux Sans Frontières. No, that would wake the old biddy up, and as old biddies in police states went, she supposed there were worse Hausvertrauensleute than Frau H. Then it occurred to her, casually, that here was Cerberus at last with all six eyes firmly closed, and Hugh gallivanting, and all she had to do was walk away. She could even try to bluff, cajole, charm or bluster her way through Checkpoint Charlie.

Strange, she had no urge to leave the hotel.

She switched off the set and went up to her room.

'If it can be arranged,' Hugh said at breakfast the next morning, 'would you go away with your friend?'

'What?'

'This came for you.' He handed Carla an envelope. She snatched it from him and screwed up her eyes to make out the postmark. Haward ath. 'From the patricidal maniac, is it?'

'Marsha,' she said, ripping open the envelope.

'Well, would you?'

Carla unfolded the letter and fixed her eyes on it without focusing.

She let her eyes move randomly over the words while she thought about what Hugh had just said. It had been so innocently put, like a staked pit covered with leaves. But what did it mean? He was trying to trap her into something, he was manipulating her. Did it have to do with Karl? Did he know about Karl? The thought that he might know was so paralysing that she couldn't trust her tongue. She hazarded a shrug, which she hoped would suggest nonchalance, that the letter was her immediate concern and more important to her than his pathetic little trap.

'One to you, Carla. I misjudged your reaction.'

She said, 'I'm trying to read this,' and found that she was reading in spite of herself, at the same time trying to work out a noncommittal answer for Hugh.

Then the letter began to register. It took over her consciousness in a series of small shocks until her mind saturated and the shocks started to spill over. She became impervious. The shocks rolled off her.

There was the postmark. Although Carla had addressed her letter to the school, she had done this automatically. In her mind Marsha was already in Geneva. Now she realised what she had known all along, that school hadn't yet broken up and wouldn't be breaking up for another two or three days. In an unreachable alternative universe and time there was a crowded Fifth Form Day Room and the end-of-term hymn, and the commonplaces of dorm gossip, delicious banalities, all of them. The letter was full of them. She might have been there, writing all this schoolgirly stuff to Marsh. It was weird.

Hugh said, 'You see, I know what you're up to.'

It rolled off, because that was the moment when it struck her that there was something horribly wrong about the letter she was reading.

At first she thought Marsha had written first, before receiving her own letter. This had been written what? . . . four days ago, on Thursday. Yes, but her own letter could have been held up, perhaps by the censor. And she'd settle for that, yearned for it to be that. And then on the second page, near the bottom, she found a reference to her own letter. 'Hotel sounds a bit yuchy,' Marsha had written, 'but what can you expect in Krautland?'

Nothing else.

Nothing about the code Carla had used.

Nothing about the tapping, about finding Karl, about being locked in. There was no reference to the broom closet, the wardrobe, Hugh's queer behaviour, to any of the *en clair* stuff. And if she'd found the code incomprehensible (forgotten it entirely—it was possible), if she'd done that why wouldn't she mention the incomprehensibility?

Marsha's letter was full of school trivia. She told some half-funny anecdotes about the Social Projects they'd been doing, gave the latest Toothy McClean catchphrase, and concluded: 'Life still crawls along here like a wounded centipede, high spot when Toothy trod in turps during old dears' flats redec. Keep exposing yourself to Fritz. Love, Marsh, Annette and the Set.'

Carla's first groping attempts to explain the madness were wild. So wild that she allowed none of them free passage through her mind.

Hugh hadn't posted her letter. But he must have, because Marsha referred to it.

Then, censorship: the obvious answer. But didn't a censored letter have black crossing-out all over it? There was no mention in Marsha's letter of deletions from her own. And it was something Marsha *would* have seized on. By the same logic, a censored version of Marsha's reply would be similarly marked. This letter was immaculate.

Carla's guesses grew wilder still.

Hugh. Hugh had steamed open her own letter and re-written it, copied her handwriting and omitted the coded section as well as some of the other content. In that case, though, why not intercept her reply to allay suspicion? If he wanted her to think nothing was amiss he would have tampered with Marsha's letter too.

Or had her message got through and drawn a compromising (to Hugh) letter from Marsh in return? And had Hugh censored, re-written *that*? Was she reading Marsha's words or a heavily Hugh-edited version of them?

Carla looked up at him.

'Anything interesting?' he said, taking a sip of coffee.

'Guess.'

III

He smiled at her. 'Guessing what's in schoolgirls' minds isn't my forte.'

'She says my letter was fascinating. Not the one you posted for me. The one I sent myself that day we got separated in the U-Bahn.'

'Ah,' he said. 'And what did you write that was so fascinating?'

'Wouldn't you like to know?'

'Not particularly, Carla.'

'Can't you guess, Hugh?'

'Knowing you, Carla, you most probably told her about my horns and cloven feet, and that I breathe fire. Oh, yes, and that I've made you a prisoner in my dungeons.' He furrowed his eyebrows in mock ferocity.

'Oh, more than that. I told her about the other thing.'

'And what might that be?'

'I thought you said you knew.'

'No. I said I knew what you were up to.'

'Okay. What's that, then?' She put on a defiant face.

Hugh put down his cup and pushed it away. 'All right. As I see it, what you are up to is some kind of elaborate charade, a game you may not even be aware you are playing—though I doubt that. It would be very sad if you weren't aware of it. The game is an obvious one. You are bored here. With East Berlin, and with the hotel. And most of all, with me. How am I doing?'

Carla felt her entire body relax, as if she'd immersed herself suddenly in a warm bath. 'Go on,' she said.

'Being bored, you want to go home. That's understandable. I'm not so insensitive—whatever you may think—that I can't see how a girl of your age might not find this the most exciting place in the world to pass a summer. Particularly if you're confined to a hotel. And not the most exciting of hotels either. Well, you know my reason for doing that.'

'Do I?'

'Oh, I think so, Carla. Come on, I'm talking to you now as one adult to another. Meet me half-way.'

'Well?' she said, grudgingly.

'After you'd already disgraced yourself on your first day here I

112

relented and let you come out with Lili and myself. We went shopping. I bought you presents, for which I got no thanks and which I still haven't seen you use. And your response? You respond by betraying my trust and sneaking away like a little guttersnipe thief, a little street Arab.' He waved away her protests. 'No. You asked to be told. Now here you are, gated because you've proved yourself unworthy of my trust, playing Cinderella. That's the game, isn't it? Lili's the ugly sister and I'm the wicked stepfather, I suppose. You mope and moan about the place day and night in the hope that I'll send you home just to get you out of my hair, or perhaps you're expecting me to relent and allow you to parade along with us, taking your nasty little pot-shots at poor Lili. And do you know, Carla, there's nothing more pitiful than the sight of you routing Lili.'

He sucked at his pipe, then as he went on talking he filled it with flake, using a practised rubbing-packing movement of his right hand that Carla watched, entranced.

'What are you? Almost sixteen, aren't you? Physically, you're undoubtedly a woman.' He stopped to light the pipe, puffing and then beginning to talk through the puffs, his voice distorted by the smoke in his mouth. It was a schoolmasterish habit she hated. Hadn't he taught in a grammar school for a while when her mother had been alive? She had a sudden deep longing for her mother that brought her to the edge of tears. She snorted to distract herself.

'Hmm. True, but it doesn't make you a woman.' He shook out the match—more punctuation. 'Because everything else about you is unmitigatedly infantile, Carla. You have a wit beyond this mentality, of course, and that's what makes your sarcasm so devastating to somebody like Lili, who is not only sensitive but hasn't the advantage of sharing your fluency in English. It isn't her native tongue. Try taking her on in German some time, though. It might be good for you.'

'Finished?'

'Almost. I've been giving you a lot of thought in the past couple of weeks, wondering what to do about you . . .'

'Buy me a dolly that pees real pee and I'll be ever so good.' She wondered if he'd developed the rub-and-poke action out of early

113

masturbation technique. This time she was going to score ten out of ten off him. He removed the pipe from his mouth and smiled.

'Illustrating the thesis, Carla? No, you won't make me lose my temper this morning. I'm feeling too buoyant. Tell me something, though. This is an earnest question. I would truly like to know if there is anything in Creation—anything at all besides gratifying your desires—that you take seriously.'

'Er . . .' she said, sucking her thumb. 'Er . . . er . . . toffee apples.'

'I didn't think there was. All right, Carla. I'm giving you the victory. Consider yourself victrix ludorum, I salute you. If I can fix it you'll be back at school for the last day of term, or else soon after. You can spend the rest of the summer in Lucerne or wherever it is with your friend, and I hope you enjoy yourself there.'

'Geneva,' she said, holding her breath, waiting for the conditions.

'I'm sure it won't seem dull to you.'

'What about that joint visa thing? You said I couldn't leave on my own.'

'That's what has to be fixed. I'll have a word with the chap I interviewed the other day, see what he can do. Seems a pretty influential body in his sphere.' He blew out a cloud of smoke.

Carla studied him. The smugness in his face reminded her of a cliché: the crooked sheriff in westerns who let his prisoner go in order to shoot him in the back. His deviousness was of the same order. He was playing his own game, a more subtle, more dangerous game than hers. He was making no conditions. That belonged to a different game. This was the come-on. She was being rushed. It was the game where you dragged on a rope so that the other person had to throw all her weight against it, and then suddenly let go. So he was using her own momentum against her. What if she let go too?

'Why the change of tactics?' she asked him. Again she got the exaggerated, raised-brow look of innocence.

'I told you. You've won. I capitulate.'

'Dead babies,' she said. 'Communication between human beings. Freedom from tyranny.'

'Too deep for me,' Hugh said. 'Sorry.'

'Things I take seriously. You wanted to know. What I'm most

114

Sometimes at night, after being with Karl, she would wonder if her own mind was sound. The question would intrude between her dozing brain and sleep, when she was most vulnerable. The difficulty was that all you had to test the soundness of your own mind was your own mind itself. To protect itself it would lie. Of course. One night she'd drifted into sleep on the thought that her entire experience in East Berlin might have been imaginary. Perhaps, in reality, there had been no tapping on the wall, no Karl, nothing sinister about Frau Holzbaum or Hugh or Lili. Perhaps because none of these things existed her letter to Marsha had contained no reference to them—which would account for the reply she'd got. And when to counter these charges against herself she had flogged her brain for proof, instances, specifics, it had shut her out and closed itself in sleep.

She dreamed she was a child again. It was a fragmented, fuzzy dream like a badly worn film. Mostly snatches of her childhood, incidents, bits of incidents, isolated images; some familiar, some forgotten. Walking with her father in smelly streets, cattle smells—a trip to a farm, perhaps. Cavernous cattle sheds with dark, hot interiors that terrified her. The noise of him fighting with her mother, waking her from sleep. Displaced images: being lifted over the heads of a crowd to see the parade. Cheering, flag-waving crowds (she'd waved a small flag herself), noise, colour—red, white and black. She'd sat on a man's wide shoulders, her bare leg scratched by his rough cheek. That hadn't been Hugh. Hugh had narrow shoulders and was always impeccably shaven. Hugh was too genteel. But in the dream he'd been her father, the same man, in every scene, the same thickly-muscled ox-like man with his low-pitched, punishing voice. A rough, unholy God. She knew the weight of his hand and the rhinoceros-hide feel of it, her real father's hand with its broken, blue-black nails, not Hugh's white and slender hand, not Hugh. She hated Hugh but she feared her father, whoever he was. Who was Hugh, then? An actor impersonating her father? There was no love between them, no intimacy, no proof that she came from his loins, only his word for it and a document or two that she couldn't even recall having seen. But when she challenged Hugh in the dream it was the other man who answered. He answered with a ringing smack across her ear that deafened her to what he said. It sounded like 'Schlampe'. Why would he call her that? She wasn't a slut.

In the morning she'd awoken to hear Hugh typing next door, and her drab hotel room, the sun obscured by buildings, was unquestionably toned in the washed-out colours of reality.

EIGHT

It was a cloudy night, so Carla had to switch on her night-light to look at her watch. 2.50 am.

She eased herself off the bed, wincing at the sound of its springs relaxing, and pulled on a sweater over her nightdress. Then she padded barefoot to Hugh's wall and pressed her ear against it. Silence. Not even his breathing.

Satisfied, Carla teased open the door to the hall, stepped out, inched it closed behind her. Long practice (she had made several raids on the kitchen over the past few days) made her efficient. Her movements were swift yet noiseless. She'd found that by arching her bare feet abnormally and putting her weight on her heels, with her toes curled to balance her, she could pass Hugh's room with hardly a sound. Walking on the balls of her feet put her off balance, and there was more chance of cracking sounds from her toe joints that way.

From the stairhead onwards there were different problems. The stone steps didn't creak, but they were narrow, and feet could slap loudly on them, toenails could click if they were too long. Carla trimmed hers every other day. She pointed her feet to the side, going down, so that they weren't at right angles to the treads. It minimised the risk of stumbling. These would be dangerous steps to fall on; unresilient stone, polished and rounded by years of constant use.

As she rounded the turn in the stairwell, eight steps from the lobby, she switched off her light and began to count off the last eight obstacles in darkness: night-sight had its uses. Then she froze, seven steps from the bottom.

Voices. She reached her hand out to touch the wall, to steady herself while she listened. She drew in her breath cautiously, through her mouth, her lips only slightly apart.

Less than three metres away somebody was talking, in the darkness.

If she turned, tried to go back, she might fall. This close, the rustle of her nightdress might be audible. She couldn't go back. Nor forward. The cold stone seemed to penetrate her feet and be working its way up through her body. Her calf muscles were trembling, but whether with tension or cold she couldn't tell. The tremor moved to her bowels, then up into her chest. Soon her entire body would be shaking violently, and he'd be able to hear the shaking, and he'd know she was there.

It was a man's voice for sure. Whispering, its tone urgent. Even in the stillness it was difficult to hear what he was saying, but the language was German. Yet only one voice. So who was he talking to?

Then she remembered.

There was a telephone in the lobby, a black pay phone tucked into that corner formed by the stairs. He was directly beneath her, talking on the telephone. In the middle of the night.

Who?

The voice was harsh and sibilant, a voice she knew but couldn't quite identify. She needed to get closer, just a little closer, and then she'd recognise it. One step would do it. His words were just, tantalisingly beyond her hearing. One step.

Bracing herself against the wall with her right arm, she took her weight on her left leg and slowly reached out and down with her right leg. The step didn't seem to be there. Praying that her bones wouldn't crack, she extended the leg another centimetre, then another, until at last there was the shock of cold stone against her skin. Sweating with the strain, she eased her weight from the left to the right side of her body.

Crack. It had been her hip joint. She waited for the whispering voice to break off suddenly, for lights to come on, for the rush of him on the stair.

But the whispering went on as before.

She could hear him now if she leaned ever so slightly forward, almost close enough to reach out and touch his head.

'Look,' he was saying, 'I'm not waiting for ever.' Then, 'Yes, I know all that, Herr Moltke . . . I know, but . . .'

Moltke. She'd heard that name somewhere before. When was that? Through the wall. Hugh had said the name and she'd heard it through the wall. No, Hugh hadn't said it. It had been that other voice, harsher, the same voice she was hearing now. God, who was he? What would she do when he hung up? If he made straight for the stairs after he put the phone down, she'd be finished. But it was his tone, rather than his words, that held her. That terribly familiar self-importance in his tone, that bullishness as he said: 'Don't forget who told you in the first place. Me. Right? Well that gives me a bit of say, doesn't it?' He sniffed. Then she heard him say, 'I don't give a tinker's how you do it, that's not my side of it. Just keep us out of it . . . No, Frau Holzbaum's got too big a yap, couldn't keep her own age secret . . . Hm . . . Might . . . Remember, she's not a bloody idiot, not like me.' Laughter. 'She's got her mother's brains. You can't just go barging in there all of a sudden or she'd smell a rat. Might even catch her in there with him. Then what? . . . No, she's sleeping, sleeps like a hedgehog.' He gave a breathy laugh. 'I bet you would. Well, a father's got rights.' More laughter.

She sensed that the conversation would end in a few seconds and turned on the stair. She began to probe with her foot for the next step up, her mind numb with shock.

She'd imagined none of it.

Hugh wasn't her father. This man was her father. The one in her dream.

And he knew about Karl.

And Moltke, whoever Moltke was, knew about Karl.

They were planning something between them, something involving her and Karl, something she would be kept out of but for which she was needed.

What?

When? 'I'm not waiting for ever,' he'd said. When?

And where did Hugh fit in to all this?

From below she heard the man's wheezy laughter again. Then the ding of the phone being replaced.

She began to race.

She slept little. Her mind kept her awake.

The most staggering thought in her head, the most persistent one, was that this whole charade must have been going on for years. Since her early childhood. For whatever reason, they'd deceived her all her conscious life, they'd kept her on ice till she could be used. And now they had a use for her. She thought she knew what that was.

The strangest thing was that the knowledge, instead of depressing her, made her feel suddenly lighter, as if she had been carrying it all this while in a box on top of her head, a deportment exercise. Now, without its weight, she wanted to breeze into the dining room at breakfast and throw the tidy little intrigue into Hugh's sickly face, calling, 'Here, catch!'

Instead, she worked hard at appearing casual, indifferent. Hugh was manic (everything going according to plan, no doubt), his movements spasmodic. He looked, Carla thought, like a man with only a short time to live who had decided to inject every atom of his vitality into every one of his actions. The acorn coffee was nectar, drinking it bliss, breathing orgasmic, being alive an act of worship in itself. He smacked his lips, a caricature of a man living life to the full.

'And how's Saint Theresa this morning?' Hugh said, then glossed: 'Child martyr.'

Carla shrugged. It was important not to seem out of character. 'Okay. Still innocent.'

'What would you like most?' he shot at her.

A nerve tingled inside her, a warning signal. 'What are you offering?'

He laughed, then bit into his roll and chewed steadily before replying. 'A day out.'

'Big deal. Where's Lili, by the way?'

Lili was another factor that didn't fit into the scheme, the one she'd worked out in the night. It explained everything. Except Lili, and Hugh, and why they were using *her*, and who she really was, and why they'd waited so long. It explained the rest, though. It would do to start with.

'She can't come with us,' Hugh was saying. 'Don't you want to know where we're going?'

'Guessing games are childish,' she said, glancing around the dining room. The same three old faces, always the same three. She suppressed a smile. She had them accounted for, at least. Fakes. This was no

121

more a hotel than it was a school or a hospital. The whole set-up was fake, brilliantly mocked up, there only for her benefit and Karl's. That much of her theory made perfect sense of a number of puzzling things. Karl, she theorised, was 'blown' (was that the word?), had been since the beginning, since before her arrival. The hotel, this improbable hotel, was a cardboard cut-out, a film set. Its sole purpose was to trap Karl and his underground organisation, the Fluchthelfer, of whom Kreismann had been one. And Carla, Carla was the bait in the trap. What they were relying on, Hugh and his masters, was that Karl would trust a naive English schoolgirl as he would trust nobody else. They had also relied on her being idealistic enough to agree to help him. She gave them full credit for that. Their psychology was faultless, and to a degree the plan had worked. But they'd made mistakes. Picking up Kreismann before she could reach him was a big mistake. Hugh's anger had first alerted her. It would have been part of his job (and Lili's?) to follow her to Karl's contacts, one by one, until they had the whole of his network in the bag. Hugh had slipped up by losing her in the U-Bahn. At first she'd been stumped by Kreismann's arrest. How had they known where to find him? Answer: they hadn't. By chance Kreismann had already been arrested, before the Stasi knew he was part of Karl's network. But they knew now, of course, now that she'd gone looking for him.

They knew where Karl would be hiding because he'd played in the cold room as a child.

And there was some kind of conflict, she guessed, between her two fathers—the real one, who'd told Moltke he wanted her kept out of things, and the fake one, Hugh, who obviously wanted her embroiled. That was the part she couldn't fathom, though. Unless Moltke was Stasi, and using her as leverage against her real father, bringing her from England expressly for that purpose, as a kind of hostage to ensure that he'd do what they wanted him to do. Which was what? Was her father a political prisoner? Then why had he sounded so pally on the phone to Moltke? It didn't work out. Whichever way she turned it, the picture refused to make sense.

Hugh broke into her thoughts. 'Well? I expected *some* reaction.' Carla shrugged again. It seemed safest. 'You are a strange girl, Carla.

I really thought you'd jump at it. Of course, if you don't want to go . . .'

'Oh, I do,' she said. Where the hell was it they were going? 'Can I wear my jeans?'

'I'd prefer a dress. I thought we might eat in one of those restaurants you're so keen on, in Ku'fü'damm.'

'Kurfürstendamm?'

'I thought it hadn't registered. West Berlin, Carla. What were you thinking about?'

'That's fantastic,' she said. What was this he was offering? A pebble wrapped in toffee paper? Would he laugh when she unwrapped it? 'The permit. You said it was a joint thing.'

'It is. Nothing to stop us both popping over for the day and coming back tonight.'

That was absurd. It was a crazy move to take her back to the west at this stage. She could run to the nearest police station, embassy, consulate, whatever, and spill the whole story. What she knew of it, anyway. At least get herself to Tempelhof and somehow bribe, beg or force her way on to the next flight back to England.

She was afraid of it.

Or had she already done her bit, played her limited role? And were they now releasing her?

That didn't tie in with what she'd overheard of the telephone conversation. God, she needed time to think about it, work it out, understand what they were doing to her. Air had got into the pump and the blood was hissing in its passage around her head.

'You'll have to give me time to change,' she said.

She sat on her bed and whipped her brain for answers. The more she worked on it the more screwy it seemed. West Berlin ought to be the last place in the world he'd take her. It wasn't safe for him, for one thing. Surely the West German intelligence services couldn't be so stupid as not to suspect him. And if they were, what was to stop her enlightening them, or MI5, or whatever the stupid thing was called? Even if they didn't believe her the suspicion alone ought to be dangerous for Hugh. No, there was something much more subtle here than she'd thought. Perhaps too subtle for Girl Wonder to work out. Oh God, why involve her in all this? None of it was her business. She just wanted to be left alone.

Automatically she began to brush her hair, then on impulse pulled it back into a bun and pinned it that way. Then she kicked off her jeans and searched through her clothes for something to wear instead. As it was a hot day she chose a thin cotton shirt and a light skirt. She checked her appearance in the bathroom mirror. No, it wouldn't do. Back in her room she thought about it. It was the skirt that was wrong. It didn't go with the bun. Quickly she unpicked the skirt's ample hem with the point of her nail scissors and tried to smooth out the crease, but without an iron it was impossible. Next, make-up. It bothered her. She wouldn't put it past Hugh to say, 'Get back upstairs and scrape that much off your face,' but so what if he did? She applied a dab of rouge to each cheek, gave the dabs a minimal rub, then for good measure thickened her waist with a folded-over sweater under the shirt. There.

She tried to remember what she had been thinking about before the dressing-up had preoccupied her. Oh, yes. Ku'fü'damm. She had been trying to work out why he was taking her out. Why was her mind so slow to function? She had to think clearly, the danger signals had to be read correctly. Something about Karl. It would mean leaving him. He was getting her out of the way so they could get at Karl. No, why should they do that unless she was being protected? Her head was spinning now. Each thought came as a separate pain. Protected, protected, protected—until the word was meaningless.

The immediate problem was to feed him, to tell him. She had to tell him what was happening, what she suspected. He had some chocolate, his water jug from yesterday. But she had to get to him. How long had she been in her room? Quarter of an hour. Too long already, he was waiting downstairs.

She found herself pulling on the wardrobe in desperation to get to Karl. A nail broke. Then one of the pencil rollers came out and had to be replaced. The shirt was already sticking to her back. Quick, quick.

But he was already calling her, Hugh, calling her name. She could hear him through the door, yelling at her.

'Coming!' she yelled back, pushing the wardrobe with all her strength.

Then he was in the room. He found her sweating, panting like a dog, the hem of her skirt beginning to curl back under her knees, her hair spilling over her eyes.

'My God,' Hugh said, 'you look ridiculous. If you think I'm taking you anywhere looking like that you must be mad.'

'Who am I?' she said.

'If you think Lili looks like that you need glasses. What's more, it's downright insulting.' When she giggled he said, 'You've got exactly three minutes to get yourself decent, and I've half a mind not to take you at all.' Then he crossed to the wardrobe and flung open its door. 'And it might help if you kept your clothes in the proper place.'

The derelict look of Bruckner's shop with the cladding nailed over it. She remembered that. And she was alert enough getting in the car.

Things began to disintegrate as they were branching off Schön-hauser Allee into Kastanien Allee. She remembered thinking that they were going in the right direction, at least, that nothing was wrong at all; remembered all that. Then she heard him telling her that it must be car sickness because she'd shown the same symptoms before in cars. The sun's rays, she heard him explain, as if to a small child, were magnified by glass, so contributing to the sickness.

He opened one of the quarter lights to let in more air. She gulped it, but felt no less dizzy. Her head was still pounding, the nausea and the prickly heat were overwhelming her, and now it was drowsiness she felt. She slipped into the relieving sleep knowing it had nothing to do with car sickness. It was the coffee. He'd put something in her coffee—a powder, a few drops of liquid—while her attention was elsewhere. She forced herself to remain conscious, jerking herself back from the edge of sleep every time she slipped because it was dangerous to be unaware of what was happening. She made a great effort to concentrate on the route he was taking, looked for street signs, places she might recognise. Was that Rosenthalplatz? Linienstrasse. For a long while it was all a blur, all the signs freshly painted, running in the rain, blurred. The Friedrichstrasse intersection with Linden passed, or was that some other busy crossing? No knowing.

She had no recollection of crossing the frontier.

It began to clear slowly, but instead of a return to full alertness she came back only to a kind of half-life, where her walking was steady and there was no dizziness or pain but an all-pervading dullness. It was as if she had been generally anaesthetised without losing consciousness. And she seemed to have lost her will. Her reactions were those of an automaton. She was aware of what she was doing, the places she went, but they registered vaguely, had no impact upon her.

They ate liver sausage in a café somewhere along Ku'fü'damm. She recognised the wide, bustling boulevard with its postered pillars and wall-mounted clocks, its pavement tables and glass-fronted shops. And there was Zigeuner-Keller, the Hungarian place, too expensive for them to eat in.

The food reminded her of Karl. Eating it, she felt a formless fear beginning to build up inside her. It had to do with Karl, and the trip with her father—why take her with him? What was happening to Karl meanwhile? She had to concentrate, had to work out what was going on.

She felt herself jump up in panic and heard breathy laughter. He was saying something she could make no sense of. His words sounded thick and seemed to come from a long way off, though he was sitting right next to her. Neither were they in Kurfürstendamm any longer; they were now sitting in one of the Zoo bars. All she wanted was to sleep, to escape the driving, screaming urgency in her brain.

Then an impression of being driven home in a van. There were no side windows, only a back window through which she could see the Tiergarten, greenery on either side of a broad avenue, then Grosser Stern, the Siegessäule painted black, then the Brandenburger Tor, roofless houses, expanses of rubble, free-standing walls . . .

Nothing after that.

'How're you feeling now?' Hugh said.

Carla had found herself lying on her bed in the hotel room. The

126

curtains were drawn, but outside it was still light. From the quality of the light filtering through, she judged it to be about six o'clock.

Soon afterwards Hugh had come in, an anxious, solicitous Hugh. Carla said nothing to him, afraid of betraying herself. Whoever this man was, he was a superb actor, and an actor would be able to recognise bad acting in others. Her mind heaved as he spoke to her about car-sickness tablets and his disappointment that her day had been spoiled. Inconsequential things, small talk, anything to distract her; or to test her reactions.

'Fuzzy,' she said.

'Sorry we had to cut it short. It's just that you were looking so green about the gills. It seemed the most sensible thing to bring you straight back. But did you enjoy it otherwise?'

Enjoy it? How the hell could she have enjoyed it? She hardly remembered any of it. Or was that the point of the question? To find out how much she did remember.

'It was okay,' she said.

'Personally, it struck me as a little brash,' Hugh said. 'Don't you think so?'

'I like brashness.'

He was pumping her, making sure the drug had worked properly. But what was the drug supposed to do? Obviously not just put her out. She was *meant* to remember going to West Berlin, and it had all been carefully staged so that she should think she had been there. She knew better. It had been too pat. No, what she'd seen through her drugged haze had been another cardboard film set, another fake environment like the hotel. They'd gone to a lot of trouble to set it up, too—the Ku'fü' that looked almost genuine but had something about it that wasn't quite authentic. What was it? She probed her memory. Drabness. They'd managed the bustle, but they'd forgotten to make it chic enough, hadn't westernised it enough. Oh, yes, they'd slipped up there. And why bring her back in a van? Because the drug had been wearing off, and from a van she would have a limited view, would think she was seeing snatches of West Berlin when in fact the snatches were all there was to see. She had never left the DDR.

Why? What was the point of it all?

127

The blanks, the blank spaces in her memory. What had happened then? She'd have to play this carefully, pretend to remember very little (which was true, anyway), acknowledge the blanks, but the one thing she had to hide was her knowledge that she'd been tricked. It gave her another tiny advantage, and the tiny advantages were mounting up. When the time came she would use them against him.

'I've got these blanks,' Carla said. Hugh began rubbing the palms of his hands along his thighs.

'Blanks?'

'Like black-outs. Bits where I can't remember anything. Did I flake out?' He was sitting on the bed, staring hard at her.

'Do you want to know something funny?' he said eventually.

'Funny-ha-ha or the other kind of funny?'

'Not funny at all, actually. Carla, I'm going to ask you a straight question and I want a straight answer. Are you taking any kind of drug?' Carla could feel her mouth fall open involuntarily in the classic gesture of shock. 'I'm serious,' he went on, interpreting her reaction as pantomime. 'You've had a glazed look all day. I have to ask it, Carla. Anything at all—sleeping pills, pep pills, anything. Are you?'

Oh, you clever bastard, she thought. You ultra-clever bastard.

'Not as far as I know,' she answered.

Hugh was constantly back and forth, checking on her, spying on her. He brought her food himself, coaxed her to eat. She nibbled, afraid of being drugged again, drank only water.

'I'm really fine,' she insisted. In the end she had to promise to see a doctor in the morning before he would leave. He lingered at the door. She yawned and closed her eyes. Why didn't he go?

'Shall I send Frau Holzbaum up to help you undress?' he said.

'I can manage. I'm not undressing with you standing there.'

'Call if you need anything. I'll be next door.'

'Just leave me alone. All I want to do is sleep.'

'Will it disturb you if I type?'

'Yes.'

'Call if you feel ill.'

Then he had gone, reluctantly. She put on her nightdress, moving heavily about the room so that Hugh would hear her. There was no sound from his room. Was he still there? Of course he was still there. He was probably ogling her through the keyhole.

She switched off the light and lay on her bed in the semi-darkness, waiting, trying to breathe in the smooth, regular rhythms of sleep.

An hour later the connecting door clicked open. It was dark now, and the open door made a brilliant rectangle in which Hugh's figure was illuminated. She heard the floorboards creak as he walked softly towards the bed.

'Carla?' It was a whisper. When she didn't respond he took another pace forward. 'Carla?'

She tried to make her voice sound as if she'd awoken from deep sleep. 'Nn? . . . Wha?' Then, as if suddenly alert, 'What is it? Hugh?'

'Did you call? I thought I heard you call.'

'You woke me up,' she said accusingly.

'I'm sorry. Go back to sleep.'

When he closed the door behind him a thin line of light showed under it. Carla fixed her eyes on it till it disappeared.

Some of the foreboding she had felt earlier in the day came back to her as she pulled away the wardrobe. She flashed her torch into the cold room, half expecting to find it empty. But Karl was there, sitting on his pile of sacks, waiting for her. He seemed undisturbed by her absence.

'I guessed,' he told her, 'that you had to go somewhere with your father. I haven't heard him either.' Carla seated herself on the sacking next to him and told him about her suspicions, her theory, her fears. She unpoured herself to him, allowing him no space to interrupt, told him about being drugged, about the blanks in her memory of the day, about the cat-and-mouse game someone was playing with both of them. And as she spoke he stared into the darkness without moving, without giving her any sign of his reaction. His body, when she touched him, was neither particularly tense nor particularly relaxed. She felt a vague uneasiness at that. It was as if he was humouring her by listening to her babblings, almost as if what she was saying was a matter of total indifference to him. The confession, the unburdening of her private terrors gave her no relief; he was taking none of it on himself. He was the man, the more worldly of them, and should have been taking the load from her. Yet he was adding to it with the weight of himself. She was having to carry him too.

'For God's sake,' she told him, 'say something. React.'

She felt his shoulders lift slightly in the gloom. 'There isn't anything to say.'

'What do we do? What should I do? Tell me. Help me, Karl.'

'We both know the end,' he said. 'Nothing we do will change it.' He must have felt her shiver because suddenly his arm was around her and he was cradling her head against his chest. He said, as if it offered comfort, 'But we'll do it anyway.'

Her thoughts kept her awake, though her body ached for sleep. It was some time after three o'clock.

She was thinking about Karl, who had wanted to make love to her. When she had refused he'd said, 'But we have to.' And childishly her response had been to flee from him back to her room, more afraid of his nonsensical words than of his touch. There had been a hint of insanity in him tonight, which on top of everything else that was happening was more than she could bear. Unless the drug was responsible—somehow continuing to distort her senses even after its numbing effects had worn off. The alternative was too unthinkable, but it was the unthinkable alternative she was thinking about; it was what was keeping her awake.

The possibility that Karl was part of their scheme after all. That he was driving her towards something . . .

She dammed the thought, diverting the stream of her mind. Think about something else. Letting Karl make love to her. Love. No, not love. Sex. Why had she refused her body to him? There was nothing precious about virginity, which, after all, was only an abstraction: a noun masquerading as a thing but not really a thing. Therefore you couldn't lose it. No 'it' to lose. Couldn't give it. 'It' wasn't a gift. Having sex for the first time was just a matter of timing, an issue of the same order as deciding when to look out your summer clothes or the right moment to . . . to what? Something mundane, anyway.

She began to drowse.

It caught her the instant before she lost consciousness. Something touching her pink nightie, lifting it. Like a strong sudden wind. Then the weight came down before she had time to push up against its force. After that it all seemed to be happening simultaneously, the weight welding her to the bed, her awareness, terrifying awareness that she wasn't dreaming this because no dream was this real, the heat of the thing on top of her, its heat and mass crushing her, the feel of its sweaty skin sticking to her, something bony grinding into her breast before it shifted to pin both her arms, numbing them, flinging them out, crucifying them; and knees on her knees, spreading her legs slowly but unclosably, a tremendously powerful hard–soft forcing thing like a padded car jack; and in her face, wherever she turned her head, the steamy foul breath, and over her mouth the rough skin of a hand, two of its fingers clipping her lips agonisingly together, a loose fingernail scraping the septum of her nose in its urgency so that her eyes ran, and the scream pressure blowing back down her throat in a choking explosion, her nose flowing too now, her back straining to arch and push off the writhing, gasping, crushing figure upon her; and something down at her tender, dry sex, pushing, forcing. The phrase 'to force an entry' touched her mind, and she grabbed for it as if it were sanity itself. It was a crime to force an entry. This thing on top of her was a criminal, then. She had a moment to recognise the shadowy outline of his face, like a bad newspaper photograph made up of too few dots, before her head was jerked sharply back into the pillow by a sudden raw agony between her legs as a hard intrusion stabbed her there, burning and scraping violently in till it met her vitals and lodged, and then it withdrew and thrust again and the blood began to flow inside her, where she could feel it hot and wet. The thing cried out at that moment—a moan, a sigh, a drawn-out aahh!—and lay still, pinning her still, inside her body still. And she refused to believe who it was who had pierced her and was now pulling himself slowly out, moistly, with the sound of wet meat slapping the block. The weight shifted. It lifted. The hand was removed. And she could breathe again.

She lay gasping, motionless, her arms and legs cruciform, lay and breathed and waited. She could hear him gasping too. In a dream this would have been the moment of waking, but there was no change in her consciousness, nor had there ever been. She lay transfixed, the wetness and pain inside her, yearning to soothe herself, to wash out the filth, but not daring to move until he had gone. She had no thoughts because there was nothing left to think about, no questions, this time, to answer. No need to ask herself if she'd imagined or dreamed or hallucinated this. It was real, it had happened, was still happening. Oh, God, make him go away, make him crawl away and die, make her father die.

Finally she heard the shuffling of his exit, his bedroom door open and close again. No lights went on.

She would not move until it got light. Until dawn she would lie perfectly still on her bed and find her equilibrium. It was over now.

But long before then she drifted into sleep. She did so wondering if it was for this that she had been brought to Berlin. The question was almost impersonal.

And when her first dream opened she knew at once that it was a dream and settled back in her sleep to enjoy the fiction, conscious that she preferred its quality to her waking nightmares.

NINE

She understood it now. Not all of it but more of it. She needed proof, any kind of proof, as much as she could get.

She stripped the bed violently, tearing a sheet in the process. Where was the blood? She had bled. She was a virgin and she'd been raped and she had bled. The sheets were rumpled but unstained. God, she was going mad. It had happened. There had to be evidence of it. There was nothing.

Wait. She'd gone to the bathroom at first light to douche herself. She had pulled off the nightdress, climbed on to the edge of the bath, and taken down the mirror that hung over the washbasin. She'd then stood the mirror vertically against the lavatory pedestal and had lain on the floor in front of it, raising her legs and spreading them so that she could check her genital area. It had been swollen and inflamed. Proof. And there was a doctor coming, wasn't there? All right, she'd show him that. The sheets could be explained. While she'd been in the bathroom Hugh or Frau Holzbaum—if she was in on it—had replaced them with another set of sheets, though not a clean pair for obvious reasons. Hugh had probably switched her sheets for those from his own bed. Good. Now they were torn she couldn't be expected to sleep on the filthy things.

Strange that she should feel as much disgust for him, almost, as for her real father, the one who'd raped her. Habit, she supposed. Well, it was time to start losing that habit. Hugh Martin was nothing to her. She knew who she was now. She'd made the connection last night, on her back, looking into the drooling face of Rudi Bruckner with his tongue characteristically between his teeth. Her father. The soldier in the photograph. No, that had probably been his father. Her grandfather. Strange, also, how clear her brain was when it should have buckled under the weight of such knowledge. There was disgust in her, yes, and loathing, but nothing she couldn't accommodate.

She had a new identity to try out now. The old Carla Martin

reactions were no longer relevant. She was Christa Bruckner now. She sounded it in the bathroom as she douched a second time. Christa. She scrubbed between her legs, welcoming the pain as a catharsis. Christa. It felt peculiar to be Christa, after being Carla for so many years. It didn't necessarily mean she was a different person, though she could become one if she wanted to, had a perfect excuse for re-shaping herself now; all it need mean was that her past was different. She wondered how old she had been when for whatever reason she'd been taken to England by Hugh Martin. In 1956? Before the Berlin Wall had gone up, when it was still possible to move freely between the occupied zones. If her birth-date was correct, and there was no reason why it shouldn't be, she would have been five in August, 1961, about the time the Wall went up. Her earliest memories of Hugh, as far as she could tell, dated from around that time. So it was reasonable to suppose she'd been taken to England then, at the age of four. That fitted with her memory of being held aloft by Bruckner to see the parade—the Germans loved parades, didn't they? She'd have been three or four years old, and a German herself.

It gave her a shock to think of herself as a German.

When she opened the door to leave the bathroom she found Hugh waiting outside with a towel over his arm.

'Early bird,' he said.

'Worm.'

'Touché. How did you sleep?'

'I had this funny dream. My father was raping me.'

His laughter sounded strained to her. 'Very Freudian. Don't go stabbing me through the braces with a carving knife, will you?'

'Now why would I want to do that to you, Hugh?' she said as she passed.

Peculiar, the way she felt towards Hugh now. The anger, the loathing ought to have gone. Yet, perhaps because she had never really known him, she found herself unable to change her feelings. He was the same Hugh, as much her father as he had ever been. Later she would decide what to do about him, and about Bruckner. Knowledge had given her superiority. She returned to her room feeling almost cheerful.

A thin man with a severe, pinched face was shown into her room by Hugh two hours later. Lili was visible behind them, looking bored.

Carla, having stuffed the sheets under her bed, was lying naked on the mattress, covered to the neck by the duvet. She watched the man uncurl a stethoscope and sign for her to pull back the duvet. She heard him say in German to nobody in particular that he couldn't examine a patient who was covered to the neck. As he spoke he pressed his warm, dry palm against her forehead momentarily, then clicked his fingers and said, 'Hand, bitte.'

Carla said, 'I've got nothing on,' and saw a slight frown pass across Hugh's face. Lili came into the room.

'I will stay,' the girl said, 'to interpret.'

Carla shook her head. The girl shrugged and went out, followed by Hugh.

'Hand,' the doctor repeated, and when Carla extended her arm grasped her wrist lightly between his fingers.

She let him sound her chest, coughed for him, showed him the inside of her mouth. He asked her in slow, careful German whether she had frequent headaches, how often and under what circumstances she felt dizzy, nauseous, what diseases she had had. She answered laconically, wondering why he'd showed no surprise at the rawness between her legs and at the bare mattress. Or was it usual in the DDR for supposedly sick people to lie on mattresses without sheets?

'What did my father tell you?' she asked him. He grunted and pulled back her eyelid. His breath smelled of mint.

When, finally, he pulled the duvet back over her and turned to go, Carla said, 'I was raped last night.'

'That would be a police matter,' he said tonelessly.

'They'd want proof.'

'Yes, they would.' He spoke without turning, still facing the door. 'I noticed the soreness,' he added, as if it had been an afterthought. 'That's no place to wash with a scrubbing brush.'

'I told you the truth.'

With a sigh he came back to the bed and removed the cover once more.

'You want me to touch you there.' It was a statement.

135

'I want proof.'

He touched her, once, lightly. Then he replaced the cover.

'Well, young lady,' he said, 'I hope you aren't disappointed. You are *virgo intacta*.'

'There's nothing wrong with you,' Hugh told her. 'It must be car sickness. Look, Lili hasn't got the car today. We're going by train. Do you want to come with us?'

'Where?'

'Factory tour. You won't find it wildly exciting, but if you want to come you can.'

'Where's her car?'

'It is not my car,' Lili said. 'It belongs to the Tourist Bureau.'

'Do I have your word you won't run off, Carla?'

'No.'

'You can't possibly prefer staying here alone. Why be so stubborn?'

'Maybe I prefer my own company.'

'Frankly, I don't know how you can stand it.'

'Perhaps,' Lili said, 'her bank manager friend in the cupboard will keep her amused.'

Karl was standing by the boarded window, his face against the rough wood. It was as if he was trying to suck the anaemic light into his lungs. Carla ran to him, pulling him round by his shoulders so that she could embrace him.

'Karl, take me too.'

'Not possible.' He straightened his arms to bring her into focus. 'You have to stay here.'

'No. I want to escape with you. I want to go today.'

'Not today,' he said.

'When, then?'

'Tomorrow.' But when she pressed herself to him again he said, 'But just me. You're safe enough here.'

'I'm not. I'm not, Karl. I'm safe with you. I don't know what's going on here. I'm afraid of it.'

'Nothing to be afraid of,' he said soothingly, stroking her hair.

'There is. Karl, he raped me.'

Her ear against his chest, she felt him stiffen, heard his heartbeat change its rhythm. 'When?' he said.

'Last night. My own father, Karl.' She waited, hating herself for testing him. But Karl said nothing. 'He's a pig,' she added.

Karl nodded. 'Tomorrow I'll send you to Schreiber. That isn't so long to wait, is it?'

'Who's Schreiber?' She didn't understand. He hadn't questioned it. Even if he was genuine she would have expected shock from him, murderous anger. And sympathy, loving solace. But there was none of that in Karl's reaction. Why was he being so cold about it? A monstrous thing had happened, and incredible as it was she was learning to accept it. But why should he? Why were his responses always so measured?

'Schreiber,' he explained, 'does what Kreismann used to do. Except that he's too mercenary for my taste. Tomorrow I'll tell you where to find him. But now I must make love to you.'

'Yes,' she said. 'You have to. If there's a baby I want to think it's yours, not his.' She shuddered. 'To me it'll be yours.'

'Even if it's born with a snout?'

She laughed. 'Even if.'

When he pressed her down on the sacking something of the night's horror returned, though it was mitigated by Karl's tenderness. 'Gentler,' she told him, catching her breath. 'I'm very sore there.' The burning pain made her bite her lip and there was no pleasure in the act. Afterwards Karl thanked her and said, 'Poor baby.'

An hour later they heard sounds from below. Something heavy being thrown across the shop, some muffled swearing. A long silence followed, during which Karl gripped her to keep her from moving. She shook her head in annoyance, to show that she knew enough to stay still.

Then somebody was calling, the voice low-pitched and unclear. It seemed to be Bruckner's voice, her father's voice, calling: 'Christa! Wo bist du? Christa!'

'You'd better go,' Karl said. 'He's missing you.'

'Frau Holzbaum's after your blood,' Hugh said at lunch.

'Must have been a small factory. You only left two hours ago.'

'Don't try and change the subject, Carla.' He broke a bread roll. 'I'm talking about your sheets. Why take out your spite on a bed sheet?'

'It tore,' she said, her mind whirling. Something was terribly wrong here. She'd stuffed the sheets under the bed. Frau Holzbaum couldn't have found them without going into her room. She'd been in the cold room all morning. The more obvious question for Hugh to ask was where she had been.

'Come on,' he said. 'Don't insult my intelligence.'

'When did she find them?'

'Ah,' Hugh said as the soup was brought in. He sniffed deeply as a bowl was placed in front of him. 'Vegetable soup. Piping hot, too. When you were sleeping. *If* you were. My guess is that you were shamming. The doctor couldn't find anything wrong with you except an over-active imagination, which apparently isn't all that uncommon in adolescent girls. Eat your soup.'

A plate of the stuff was steaming in her face. She felt suddenly ravenous. When she was sleeping, he'd said. When the hell was that?

'What's it got in it?'

'What's usually in vegetable soup?'

'Water.'

'Ninety-nine percent. But I can tell you,' he said, sipping some of the broth off his spoon, 'the other one percent tastes excellent.'

Carla tried a tentative mouthful. Suppose Frau Holzbaum was on her side, conniving with her, complaining about the sheet but not letting on to Hugh that she'd been missing from her room. Suppose there was an ally in Frau Holzbaum. And an enemy in Karl, who hadn't batted an eyelid at hearing her called Christa. She hadn't worked that out yet, hadn't had an opportunity to confront Karl with it yet. How did Karl know who she was unless Bruckner or Moltke had told him? He said he'd got in through the shop, so maybe . . .

'Carla,' Hugh's voice broke in, 'you're making a pig of yourself.'

She stopped eating, suddenly aware that she'd been spooning the soup into her mouth like a starving person.

'Starving,' she said, her mouth still full of the thick broth.

'Well, slow down, for heaven's sake. The English aren't famed for much abroad these days, but we still have an international reputation for good table manners.'

We? She was on the brink of saying it. We? Nothing English about Christa Bruckner. Just an English public school overlay. She wondered what his reaction would be if she told him how much she knew already. It was tempting, if only to disturb that calm of his, that insufferable composure that he wore like a white linen suit. She slurped more soup.

'Ah, what's this?' Hugh said. He was chewing reflectively, his head slightly inclined. 'Beef?' Carla's spoon came to rest in her bowl as she watched him. 'No.' He smacked his lips appraisingly. 'Pork, I think.'

It came out in a thick stream, as from the sump of her innards; a jet of it, into her bowl, across the table into his bowl, on to the floor. As she turned, helpless, it sprayed in different directions, like a strafing of automatic fire. A gout of the soup-vomit landed on Hugh's forehead and ran down his nose, but after the first unavoidable burst he seemed to have decided that there was no point in moving. He sat solemnly through the torrent, like a man with a lot to say patiently waiting for another speaker to finish.

When finally there was only a thin, almost transparent dribble coming from Carla's mouth, Hugh said quietly: 'Go to your room, please, Carla. Wash yourself first.' He wiped his face carefully with his table napkin, then without a change in the modulation of his voice, said, 'You have just bolted and regurgitated your last meal in this dining room.'

She had the kitchen and the shop confused in her memory for some reason. She had a feeling that the shop could be reached through the kitchen, but she wasn't sure which of them she wanted. She hesitated at the swing doors. If it was Rudi Bruckner she was going to see, she could go through the customers' entrance in the street. Frau Holzbaum wasn't guarding the door. Frau Holzbaum was probably in the kitchen preparing dinner. But maybe it was Frau Holzbaum she wanted. The need to talk to somebody, to somebody other than Karl or Hugh, had brought her down to the lobby. The conviction that if she didn't talk about what was happening to her she'd soon pass beyond the point where it mattered and would no longer care. Perhaps, if it was Frau Holzbaum she saw, she could appease the old woman by offering to pay for a new sheet. What if it was Bruckner? What would she say to him? That she knew she was his daughter and wanted to introduce herself? Tag, Vati. Long time, no see. She giggled at the thought of saying that. It was such an incredible situation, being Christa Bruckner when she knew she was Carla Martin, when everyone else—Marsha, Toothy McClean, everyone—knew she was Carla, that she ought to be laughing it off. Why wasn't she writing witty letters home about it? That was easy to answer. Because that world wasn't real. This was home. This was where she belonged.

She pushed open the swing doors.

The kitchen was a surprisingly small one for a hotel with perhaps thirty rooms and four storeys. Nobody was there, though an enamel pot was steaming away to itself on the black-leaded range and an assortment of diced vegetables, as for a stew, lay on the heavy old wooden table in the centre of the room. A knife lay beside them. She had the sense of entering a room where a small fire—one that had fizzled out on its own—had panicked the occupants into fleeing. The cook should have been there, and Frau Holzbaum to supervise.

She looked around. The kitchen was windowless, but there was an air vent to the street, with a noisy electric fan in front of the grille. Yes, she'd noticed that from outside. The corrugated iron sheeting began just a few centimetres beyond it. Which meant the shop would be on the other side of the far wall, where the dresser was. She walked over to it and tapped on the wall. It gave out a hollow sound. Boarding only. The shop was connected to the kitchen, then. She'd thought so. She wondered if her father was on the other side of those wall boards now, working at his block. She couldn't hear anything. She put her ear to the steam-coated wall, but that only magnified the bubbling of the stewpot.

She moved across to the table, idly, unsure what to do next. She picked up the knife and examined it. The grip was of black hardwood, unvarnished and greasy, but comfortable in the hand as a good knife should be. The blade was of unpolished steel, twenty centimetres long and wedge-shaped—tapering along both its width and its thickness to a fine point—its edge honed concave and razor sharp. She knew from the feel, the balance of the knife, from its heft, that it was a fine piece of steel. Her touch became caressing, covetous. She wanted that knife. Wanted it under her pillow.

Then the door swung open and Frau Holzbaum came in. When she saw Carla holding the knife she stopped suddenly. Carla at once replaced the knife on the deeply scored wooden table and smiled. 'I wanted to see you about the sheet,' she said in German.

'What are you thinking of doing with that? Cutting up your mattress?'

'I was only looking at it.'

'You know how much sheets cost?'

'I've got money,' Carla said, disappointed because the conversation wasn't pleasant. She wanted it to be pleasant. 'When were you in my room?'

The old woman snorted. 'This morning. I found the sheets under your bed, don't worry. You didn't hide them from me. But I also went back this afternoon and looked in your wardrobe. I know about you. Think you've been so clever, but I know about you.'

'What are you going to do?'

'You'll find out. When your father comes back you'll find that out. I'm reporting it. Don't think I won't.'

'Which one?'

'All of it, that's which one.'

'Which father?'

'What?'

'My English father or my German father?' But she could see by Frau Holzbaum's eyes that she didn't understand. How could she even begin to make this old woman who smelled of cabbage understand what was going on? She felt suddenly overpowered by weariness, hopeless. Drowning, she was too exhausted to raise her hand to summon a rescuer. Let the waters close over her head, let her have peace. She took a step towards Frau Holzbaum. The old woman backed away a pace.

'Please, help me, Frau Holzbaum. Please.'

'Get out of my kitchen.'

'I'm Christa, Frau Holzbaum. Won't you help Christa?'

'Christa?' And she could see that something had come into the old woman's face that hadn't been there before. What was it? Sadness, pity, something deep. It was there in her eyes. Christa was a nerve she could touch and go on touching, probing at till Frau Holzbaum remembered.

'It was a long time ago,' she said. 'I don't expect you to remember me.'

But Frau Holzbaum was screaming. 'Get out! Get out!'

And the look wasn't pity after all, it was terror.

Hugh said, 'Tomorrow's your last day in East Berlin, Carla. The rest of your meals will be sent up. And don't bother going into your Prisoner of Chillon routine because it's no longer necessary.'

His right ear, Carla noticed, was bright red. Half an hour or so earlier she had seen him drive past in the Volkswagen. Now he was back with a red ear.

'I couldn't arrange a flight for the morning,' Hugh went on, 'but you'll be on BEA 1224 leaving Tempelhof at 4.30 tomorrow afternoon. Allison and Peter will meet you at Heathrow. If they want to let you, and if her family will have you—which is more to the point —you can go to Switzerland with that friend of yours. Whatever you like. It doesn't concern me.'

He's been taking orders by phone, she thought. Orders to put everything forward. That was why he'd gone out instead of using the phone in the lobby.

'Suits me,' she said dully. She was going to give nothing away either. That was a decision she had made. He was rushing her, trying to panic her, to cut her off from Schreiber—how did he know about Schreiber? All right, she'd put her own schedule forward and go to Schreiber tonight. It would be too risky by daylight. Meanwhile, she had to act the dummy, giving the orthodox, expected answers when he pressed the appropriate buttons—become an automaton, volunteer nothing, suppress herself, hide inside herself. It was the way to survive. Survival was the game now.

'I haven't told Peter and Allison about the thefts,' Hugh was saying. 'So you needn't unless you want to. Your soul might benefit from a bit of confession. You need something. Don't look so worried, I'm not going to lecture you. I'm too exhausted by you, frankly, Carla. My God, you've been inventive, I'll give you that. I've also managed to persuade Frau Holzbaum not to take the thing any further, and believe you me, she's an expensive woman to reason with. Carla, I'd appreciate some kind of response from you to all this.'

What thefts was he talking about? The food she'd filched from the kitchen night after night? They'd have to number individual crumbs to notice those losses. 'I was hungry,' she said.

Hugh snorted. 'I take back what I said about your inventiveness. Tumblers and a jug? Cups? She caught you in the act of taking a kitchen knife.'

Carla looked hard at him but saw only cold, controlled anger. It wasn't enough. He knew about the jug and the cups. Did that mean the old cow had taken stock suddenly? If not, it meant the things had been found, in which case it was all over, everything. Those things were in the cold room, with Karl. But then she'd have known. There would have been droves of police cars outside, a crowd. There was nothing.

'I'll need to know from Miss McClean if you have a history of kleptomania.' He changed his tone, became pleading. 'Why, Carla? And don't give me any of that psychiatric twaddle about cries for help. Why do it? Why two of everything? And a kilo of butter. I'm sorry, I don't see anything to smile about. The stuff's like gold here.'

'Frau Holzbaum on the make,' Carla said. He was fantastic, so fantastically convincing she almost believed he was genuine. Oh, if only she could believe that.

'That doesn't explain a damn thing and you know it. I suppose it was Frau Holzbaum who tore your sheets.'

'No, I did that.' After someone changed them. She thought it and was on the verge of voicing the thought when she remembered what

143

she had decided. An automaton. Volunteer nothing. Bluff, but never call.

'One thing puzzles me,' Hugh said. 'Why leave the sheets under your bed instead of hiding them in the wardrobe with the other things?'

Being watched all the time, having her food brought up (she ate none of it) made her feel her life was circular, a model railway track. As the train moved time passed, but every so often the same bit of scenery would come round again. Yet she could never quite remember what lay ahead, though she knew she must have passed that way before. She was living her life as if it had become a habit she couldn't break. That was an odd feeling, but not as odd as being told she could simply fly away tomorrow. As if it were so easy that all she had to do was step on board an aeroplane.

Meanwhile she would play the dummy, let them underestimate her. When Hugh was with her she would say little, answer his questions but offer nothing, so as not to anger him. And when she was alone she wouldn't even bother to check whether they locked her in. She knew now that her only way out was through Karl, and as soon as she got the chance, tonight, she'd go to him. And all the while there was the comfort of his baby, already beginning to form inside her. It would resemble Karl, she was sure, but not too obviously. That would be dangerous. She refused to let herself dwell on that, and when the thought insisted on invading her mind she would have to wrench her mind away to something nice instead, like mountains with snow on them and the fresh footprints she'd leave in the snow one day.

The dark was what she was waiting for. The loved–hated dark, that hid the watchers from her but also concealed her from them. A whore, a traitor, serving and loving any master. When it was dark the last stage would begin of the race she was running; the last act of the play in which they were all acting. Herself. Her father. Karl. Moltke.

Timing was everything. If she went too late, a girl alone on the streets at night, she would attract attention. Too early and the night would not provide cover. Half past nine seemed a good hour.

At nine o'clock she pulled away the wardrobe and entered the cold room. Karl was asleep and had to be shaken awake.

'I'm going now,' she said. 'Do you understand? I've got to go to Schreiber tonight.'

She saw that he was disoriented, unsure of himself. He groped for her, and she let him take her hand. 'What difference do you think it will make?' Karl said. She heard sucking sounds as he moistened his dry lips, then something like a sob. 'We can't beat them.'

'Stop snivelling, for God's sake. Tell me where to go.'

'He lives in Rummelsburg. But there's no point.'

'Just give me the address. What do we want?'

'Full set of papers. Passport, identity card, labour card, ration card —the lot. He won't need photographs yet. He'll know. He's done it all before.'

'Where do I find him?'

'Kaskelstrasse 26. There's a brother in the house, so make sure it's Wilhelm Schreiber you see. He's about fifty, wears glasses—half steel rims. If you want to check him ask about his son, Hans. Say you know someone who went to school with him at the Gymnasium. Ask him who taught Hans his Physics.'

'Who did?'

'Man name of Epstein.'

'Epstein,' she repeated. 'Kaskelstrasse 26. Wilhelm Schreiber, son Hans. Got it.'

'Look,' Karl said, 'I don't want you to go now. Go tomorrow if you have to, but don't leave me now. A day won't make any difference.'

'Which station do I want?' she said. 'Rummelsburg?'

'No, Ostkreuz. It's more direct, on the Ringbahn. Please, I want you here with me for the time we've got left. I want us to learn to love each other.'

'Stop being a big baby, Karl.' She checked her watch with her flashlight, and when she saw him look longingly at the flashlight she gave it to him. 'I'm not afraid of the dark,' she said.

'When are you going?'

'Now.'

145

'Through the shop?'

'Of course.'

'Kiss me first.'

She bent and kissed him, then pulled away and without looking back crossed to the wooden stairway which led down to the shop.

PART THREE

The wood was old and wormy and the stairs creaked alarmingly. At the bottom she had some difficulty with the door, which had warped into its frame. Karl came down to help her and together they managed to get it open. He touched her forehead once with his lips before returning up the stairs.

The shop, which had closed hours before, was almost totally dark. Without her torch she had to find her way by touch alone through the refrigerated store-room at the back of the shop. Touching against something chill and moist, she recoiled in horror, then realised in the same instant what it was. A carcase. She patted it as one pats a sleeping dog and slipped between it and another dead animal hanging beside it. She was moving like a sleepwalker, with both arms extended at shoulder height, feeling her way. The wall, along to the steel door; she slid her hand down and turned its handle.

She was now in the shop proper. She touched the counter with her left hand. Cold, greasy marble. Her right hand, groping, encountered the deep scores of the wooden chopping block, passed over it with care in case a knife had been left there. Another ten paces brought her to the front door, easy to see because it had two glass panels that let in light from the street.

Here she anticipated problems with the lock. Meat was valuable. The door had two bolts and a police-approved lock. Standing on her toes, she was able to undo the top bolt without difficulty. The bottom bolt was stiffer—this door, too, had a warp in it. She had to kneel on the sawdust floor and press her weight against the door to pull that bolt, and it came free slowly with a grinding sound that seemed to fill the shop. For several seconds she waited, completely still, listening. Her own breathing was the only sound, though she fancied that her blood was pulsing noisily through her taut body.

Now the lock. It was a double lock; one half could be opened from inside by turning a small lever, but simultaneously the other, mortised part had to be opened with a key. That was the problem. That should have been the problem—the key shouldn't have been in the lock. Incredibly, it was.

Oversight?

Or had it been left that way on purpose, to make it easier for her? At that moment she was tempted to go back, to abandon the whole thing. Then she reasoned it out: if they knew enough to set a trap, what did it matter if she was caught in it today or tomorrow? And if it wasn't a trap but a genuine oversight, how criminally stupid it would be of her to waste the opportunity.

She pulled the shop door open very carefully, reaching up at the same time to muffle the clapper of its bell, and stuck her head out into the street.

Nothing. No-one. The sun had recently set, and although not yet totally dark, the street lay in deep shadow. If somebody was hiding there, waiting for her, there were enough places where he could be concealed.

Once outside, she closed the door behind her in a single swift movement. No way of locking it, but if he'd forgotten the mortise—genuinely—then he could think he'd forgotten to lock up at all. Only a patrolling policeman or a lucky thief would find out otherwise, and she'd be back within a couple of hours to slip back in and bolt the door the way she'd found it.

The streets were empty and silent, which was bad because it made her conspicuous and liable to be spot-checked by the police. As she walked she tried to recall what Karl had said about how you could tell if you were being followed. One of the things you did, she remembered, was to stop suddenly and listen. Only if the person following had lightning reactions could he stop in time to prevent your hearing his steps. She made a sudden stop. She listened, heard nothing but a cat mewing from a doorway, walked on again. Shortly afterwards a man passed her on the other side of the road, but he went on without even glancing her way. After turning into Wichertstrasse she stopped a second time, then again a few hundred metres further on, swinging round quickly. She saw and heard nobody. It made her feel foolish, wheeling round like that in an empty street. It was a great relief, then, to come out into Prenzlauer Allee and see a few people moving about, though there was no traffic.

It was easier to keep a check on the station platform, since she was the only person waiting for a train in the direction of Ostkreuz. A notice chalked on a board said that although trains were running abnormal delays could be expected on the Ringbahn. She paced the platform. Then she heard boots ringing on the iron steps and a soldier came on to the platform. She stiffened as he began to walk towards her, but he seemed to change his mind and crossed to the other platform. When the next train pulled in, bound for Schönhauser Allee, he boarded it.

Her own train arrived ten minutes later. It was a painfully slow journey. The train made frequent stops between stations. Once it waited a long time on the stretch of line she hated most, where the line ran by the sheds of the central cattle market, row after row of dark shapes in neat, ordered units, the shapes of death. She turned her back to them in the silence, quivering.

From Ostkreuz she walked briskly through the darkened streets. It was already late now, and her urgency made her want to run. But in this quiet neighbourhood at night it would be conspicuous to run. She forced herself to seem unhurried but purposeful to any watching eye, as if she was late getting home and knew it.

Without the night-sight she'd developed in the cold room she doubted that she would have found Kaskelstrasse. It began in the middle of nowhere, at the edge of a large patch of open ground, and as she passed several ruins she had a short-lived but powerful presentiment that Herr Schreiber's house would turn out to be one of those ruins.

Then she found the place. It was a five-storey walk-up of sooty brick with ornate window surrounds, once white and elegant, now the colour of slate. The bell marked Schreiber was the old-fashioned kind that had to be pulled rather than pushed. She heard it ring distantly and had to fight an impulse to run away, the child awakening the sleeping giant. In the few seconds that she waited she was assailed by all the fears of her childhood, an infinity of terrors that froze her to the step, and she found herself wondering how she had come to be here and how often she would have to come here again.

The door was opened by a fresh-faced young man who smiled pleasantly at her and gave a little bow from the waist. 'Come inside, please.'

She hesitated. He could be the brother, but somehow she didn't think so. Her instincts made her scalp prickle against him, and there was something familiar about him that worried her. She didn't know the Schreibers. There should be nothing familiar about this man.

'Is Herr Kuhn in?' she said. She had to get away, pretend to have the wrong house.

'Come in, please, my dear young lady,' the man said, which amused her because 'gnädiges Fräulein' was such a comical expression.

'Everything's all right,' he told her when they were inside the house. 'I'm Hans Schreiber. You want to see my father.'

'Is he in?'

'I'll fetch him for you. Does he know you? Who shall I say is calling?'

'He doesn't know me. Actually, I've come for a friend of mine.'

'I'm forgetting my manners. Let me offer you something. Coffee?'

She shook her head. 'Don't I know you?' she said. 'Didn't you used to live in Prenzlauer?'

'No, we've always lived here.'

'I thought you must have gone to the Gymnasium in Prenzlauer. I assumed that was where Karl knew you from.'

'Karl,' he said. 'Now which Karl would that be?'

'You were in his Physics class, weren't you? What was that chap's name who taught Physics? Karl said you both used to tease him rotten.'

'Ah,' he said, smiling broadly. 'Apple-Head. Newton. You see? We called him Apple-Head. Because he taught Physics,' he added, 'not because his name was Newton. I'll get my father.'

'You're probably thinking of the one who left,' she said. 'The Jew. Grünwald.'

'Was he the one Karl said we used to tease?'

'No. That was Ebert.

'Ah, yes. Ebert. Mad as a loon, old Ebert.'

'Look,' she said, 'it's really too late to be bothering your father. It's not that important. I'll call back tomorrow.'

'You're quite a bright girl,' the man said. 'Why do you want to see Herr Schreiber?'

She turned towards the door, but he jumped quickly in front of her.

'I'll come back tomorrow.'

'My dear young lady, we've established that I'm not Hans Schreiber. No need to keep up the pretence. My name is Moltke.' He pulled a wallet from his jacket pocket and flipped it open. She glimpsed a flash of white card behind cellophane. 'Secret State Police.'

Another man had come into the room. While Moltke pulled on a black leather coat the second man asked her name and address. She answered mechanically, her mind a vacuum. She heard Moltke say, 'Send for him,' and they waited while the second man made a tele-phone call from the hall. After that she was taken out to a car and driven back towards the city.

Neither of them spoke to her on the way. She concentrated on trying to identify the streets they passed through, but the darkness of the city made it impossible.

Then she was led into a large building that streamed with unbear-able light. There was a marble-floored hallway overhung with chrystal chandeliers, and a grand staircase also of marble. She was taken up and into an opulently decorated room with thick red carpets and oak-panelled walls. Moltke treated her with exaggerated polite-ness. He invited her to sit in a deep club chair, while he seated himself behind a mahogany desk. When he spoke it was in patient, controlled tones.

'Your father will be here soon. Relax. Tell me why you went to see Schreiber.'

Her mind refused to function. She stared dumbly at him. This man knew everything. He knew who she was, and about Schreiber, and why she'd gone to Schreiber. What did he hope to gain by interrogating her? And why here in this beautiful room instead of some filthy, rat-infested cellar? 'You know why,' she said.

'You mean Karl,' he said. 'Friend of a friend and all that. Then why ask to see Hans' father?'

It made no difference what she said. She summoned an easy lie. 'Karl said old Schreiber was someone kind who'd listen if you had troubles.'

'I'm kind. I'm a good listener. So talk to me, my dear young miss. Tell me who Karl is first of all.'

'I don't know his other name. He's just someone I met in the park. He gave me one of his sandwiches, then it got to be a regular thing for a few weeks. I haven't seen him for ages.'

'Yes, I see. And these troubles you went to talk over with kind old Wilhelm Schreiber?'

'It's my father,' she said. 'I can't stand the way he treats me. I just wanted someone to moan to, sort of like an uncle.'

Moltke was nodding as if he understood perfectly. 'Does he beat you?'

'And he mauls me.'

Moltke tut-tutted sympathetically. 'He sounds like a pig,' he said, 'a perfect pig.' A telephone rang on Moltke's desk. 'Send him in,' he said into the phone.

A few moments later her father came into the room. He looked unperturbed, she thought, as if he'd been waiting all along for Moltke's call but now had to go through the motions of showing anger.

'What's she doing here?' her father said. 'How did she get out? I locked that little bitch in her room.'

'Herr Bruckner,' Moltke said, 'do you know anyone named Schreiber?'

'No, and what's she been up to? Gallivanting little trollop. It's nothing to do with me, nothing she's mixed up in. I'm an Old Fighter, me. Four-figure Party number.'

'I know,' Moltke said.

'Little snot,' Bruckner said. 'Must've got herself a key from somewhere.'

'Then I suggest you change the lock, Herr Bruckner.' Moltke smiled. 'Now you can take her home. I've no charge to bring against her.'

'Who's this Schreiber, then?'

'No connection relevant to my investigations of Herr Schreiber has been established with your daughter. Please try to keep her home at night. Good night, Herr Bruckner. My dear young lady.'

He took her home in the van. Its meaty smell, together with her fear, made her feel sick. She struggled to control her stomach.

'You're really going to get it this time,' her father said, but her mind was far away.

Did they or didn't they know where Karl was hiding? If they knew, why hadn't they arrested her? Yet he'd said he'd locked her in, and he might just be dense enough not to realise that she had got out through the old store-room and the shop. In which case the shop would have to be locked again before he opened up for business in the morning. If he found that door unbolted even he couldn't fail to make the connection between her escape route and the old cold room behind her bedroom wall—a connection Moltke had probably guessed vaguely at without knowing the shop's history or its geography. But even without knowing that, Moltke must be on to her. That she had somehow got out of a locked bedroom and gone by night to a known forger must suggest to Moltke that she was hiding a fugitive, inevitably a Jew. And it was surely no coincidence that Moltke had been 'investigating' Schreiber on the very night she turned up there. So how did he know? She hadn't been followed. She must have been overheard discussing Schreiber with Karl.

It was only a matter of time, then, before they were both picked up. Moltke, she supposed, would keep a day and night watch on her for a while, and one night, when it pleased him to, he would come and take her and Karl away. Karl would be sent to a camp in the General Government, in Poland somewhere. She'd heard talk about those places, the things that were done in them. Horst, one of her father's boozing pals, had done a stint in one of the camps and liked to shoot his mouth off about them. As for herself—she would be hanged. They hanged you for sheltering Jews. It was done on the quiet, and nothing ever appeared in *Völkische Beobachter* about it. She accepted it, though Karl might not.

155

Meanwhile, did Moltke really expect her to lead him to another forger, and then another? To a whole trail of people like Schreiber? He was no fool, and he knew she wasn't a fool either. Only her father, pig in the middle, was a fool. But he wouldn't be touched by the business. He knew Goering, was an Old Fighter from the pre-'33 days. None of it would stick to him.

'And I want that sodding key, you cunning bitch,' he was saying.

'When we get home,' she told him. 'Can't you go faster?' A vague, pathetic half-hope had formed in her tired mind that they might get back before Moltke had time to send his leather-coat boys to watch the street; that she and Karl might make it out tonight, catch Moltke off balance.

'Shut your trap. It's the black-out, isn't it?'

She caught him off guard as he was steering the van to the kerbside outside his shop. In a single movement she threw open the door and jumped out. She started running away from the apartments, hoping to draw him off, hoping he'd be dull-witted enough to chase after her. A car she hadn't seen before, a black Mercedes, was parked further along the street. As she ran past she glimpsed the figures of two men inside it. Neither of them seemed to be looking at her, but she knew that Moltke was inescapable, and the imbecilic notion of outrunning him went out of her head. All she wanted to do now, though, was shake off her father long enough for her to double back and slip in through the shop. Without slowing, she turned her head. There he was, the beer-bloated pig, lumbering after her with blessed predictability.

She turned the next corner and raced for the crossroads. Three options. Instead of taking one of them she ducked into a doorway and waited for him to run blindly, unthinkingly past like the oaf he was. She even had to allow herself the faintest of smiles when, twenty or thirty seconds later, he did exactly that. She saw him hesitate momentarily to regain his breath, and then he was off, having chosen the option to the left. With luck he wouldn't know he'd been duped till he reached Prenzlauer Allee.

Once inside the shop she bolted the door top and bottom, breathing heavily. Then, instead of returning through the cold room she entered the apartment block by the door behind the counter. This led to a common entrance-way. The stone staircase to the Bruckners' apartment was here, and the doors to four ground-floor flats.

As she started up the steps one of those doors opened. The caretaker's wife, a sour-faced woman in her early forties, poked her head out.

'Christa,' she said, 'I thought I heard someone in the shop. Was that you?'

'Yes, Frau Holzbaum. Daddy wanted change out of the till.'

'I don't like money left there over night.'

'I'll tell him,' Christa called, climbing the stairs.

Frau Holzbaum shouted after her: 'And I don't like these comings and goings after midnight. Tell him that too, please. If it isn't air-raids it's the tenants.'

Her room was unlocked. He must have checked on her when he got the phone call and forgotten to lock the door again. Or thought that there was no point in relocking it.

Hurriedly she packed a suitcase, deliberately leaving the room in disarray. Frau Holzbaum would tell him she'd been up to her room. She wanted him to think she had come down again. If he didn't know about Karl it was vital not to make her disappearance a mystery so that his slow brain wouldn't connect her going with the old cold room. She listened from the stairhead, then looked out of her bedroom window. There was no sign of him. He'd probably given up the chase and gone off somewhere in search of drink. His Party badge could get him booze at any hour.

Satisfied, she pulled away the wardrobe and went to Karl.

'Well?' Karl said.

'We're dead,' Christa answered. 'The Gestapo were waiting.'

'Oh, God.'

'It was God who turned us in,' she said with a laugh. 'I told you not to trust in Him. He turned us in to a very sweet man named Moltke. There's a car out there now with two men in it.'

'What do we do? Christa, what do we do?'

157

'Nothing we can do. Wait.'

'What about your father?'

'I don't know about him. He may not know yet.'

'Oh, he doesn't know. Believe me, he doesn't know. I'd be chopped into little pieces by now if he did. What's the Gestapo waiting for?' When Christa told him what she thought Moltke was waiting for he said, 'That doesn't add up. There's only Arnold Kreismann, and I don't even know his address except that it's somewhere in Tauben-strasse. What I know about the underground your Moltke could get out of me in ten seconds if he wanted to. In one of those basement cells under the Prinz-Albrechtstrasse. I'm not a very brave man, Christa.'

'That's another thing,' she said. 'I wasn't interrogated. Not the full works, anyway.' Then immediately, 'Shh.'

Rudi Bruckner was in her room. They could hear him throwing things about in temper, shouting, 'Where's that bitch gone now?' A knocking sound came from below and Bruckner called, 'Shut up, you dried-up twat.' A door slammed, and afterwards it was silent again behind the wall.

Karl said, 'Where's he gone?'

'Either to beat Frau Holzbaum's brains in or off to some Kneipe to get pissed. Hopefully both.' Then she added, 'Funny. I always thought Frau Holzbaum would be the one. She's always denouncing the tenants for not giving the "German Greeting" or fiddling the rations, stuff like that. Finding a "U-Boat" in her block would give her an orgasm.'

'You could always do that,' Karl said. 'Denounce me.' After a pause he added, 'That may even be what they're waiting for.'

Later, when it was light enough, Karl went to the window and tried to see through a gap between two of the boards. It was im-possible to tell whether the Mercedes was still there, but the Gestapo's preferred hour for arrests had passed and nothing had happened. Neither of them had slept during the night. At about two o'clock they'd heard Bruckner come in drunk and crash about for a while in his room. He'd checked Christa's room too. They'd heard nothing from him since.

At seven o'clock Christa went down to the shop and came back with a carving knife. 'Look what I've got,' she told Karl.

'Oh, Christa,' he said in quiet despair, 'that really is absurd.'

'It's for him. I'm going to stick him. When they come for us that's the first thing I'm going to do.'

'What will they do to you? I mean, do you think . . . ?'

'They'll hang me,' she said matter-of-factly.

'Defeatism isn't like you.'

'You sound like Frau Holzbaum. She's still waiting for the Third Front to open.'

Somewhere outside a car started up. It idled for a few moments before driving away.

'Changing of the guard,' Karl said with a smile.

'I'm going to look.'

The light was hurtful to her eyes as she pushed the wardrobe on its improvised rollers. Her bed was the first thing she focused on. The sheets, slept in but recently laundered and still showing the creases, were turned back, inviting. Now the lack of sleep caught up with her. Her legs were wobbly and her movements to the window were a series of jerks. Like a drunk, she thought. And yes, the car was gone, no cars at all in the street. She had to get back to tell Karl, but the bed, just to feel its softness for a moment, only a moment's rest . . .

She sensed that something was wrong the moment she opened her eyes. She'd overslept. Karl was waiting. How long had he been waiting? She reached out automatically for her watch, but it had stopped. Now her senses were screaming at her, alerting her. Something else, something else was wrong. What? Everything, everything. The dream.

What dream?

She was fully awake now, sitting upright in her bed. Impressions flashing like a strobe light, stunning her, charging her brain with unbearable voltage.

She was in her nightdress, her watch on the dressing table, the dark clothes she'd worn last night flung carelessly over the chair, the sound of heavy traffic outside, distant.

159

What dream? Dreams were vague, insubstantial things—real enough to the sleeper but instantly gone once the sleeper woke, their world flimsy in recollection. Sometimes she could remember the outline of a particularly vivid dream, sometimes a few details, but the dream world had boundaries—border posts, yes border posts you had to cross. You could no more mistake a dream for reality than you could mistake East Berlin for West. The thought triggered off another staccato burst of memory images. Hugh taking her to West Berlin, a fake West Berlin. An artificial environment she'd been supposed to find credible under the influence of drugs. Was that what they'd done last night? This time there were no gaps. It was all there—Moltke, Bruckner, the ride home ('home'?) in the van, Frau Holzbaum, a younger Frau Holzbaum asking her about money being kept in the shop, Karl, the parked Mercedes. All of it. And the last thing she remembered, the last thing she had done was to check that the car had gone. And it had.

She dashed to the window. Hugh's red Volkswagen was parked immediately below, the only car in the street. It hadn't been there last night, but how could it have been? Last night was supposed to be 1944.

Oh, God, what were they doing to her? What did they want? *How* was it being done? How?

She dressed hastily in the dark green sweater and skirt that she had worn last night to go to Schreiber. There were no other clothes on the chair, but that was a minor worry compared with everything else she had to think about. What was first? She found she was literally turning in circles, her eyes searching every quarter of the room as if the room itself might provide a clue, a suggestion as to what she should do first. Karl. Karl was first. Of course, Karl.

If he was there.

If he had ever been there.

She ran her fingers lightly over the dark wood of the wardrobe. What if it didn't budge when she pulled on it? Her palms were suddenly wet, unable to grip the wood. They slipped off when she pulled. It's sweat, she told herself. It won't move because of the sweat on my hands. She rested her face against the cool wood, and was in that position when Hugh came into the room.

'Ah, you've been busy,' he said. 'Sleep was what you needed.'

'What time is it?'

'Just gone half eleven.' He nodded at the room. 'I see you've packed.'

'Packed?'

'Where's your case? I'll take it down to the car if you like.'

'Oh,' she said. 'No, it's all right.'

'In here, is it?' She felt him close to her. His hand was on the latch of the wardrobe. She tried to think of words to say that would stop him, but her mind was a void. Then the wardrobe door was open and Hugh was reaching inside, pulling something out. Her vanity case, bulging. 'Good girl,' Hugh said.

ELEVEN

There were moments of great clarity, when she could reason, pose questions, stumble towards solutions, pinion her writhing mind for a brief, lucid space while she tested reality; and there were times when she gave up struggling, gave herself up to it—whatever it was—and let her mind submit, uncaring, to violation.

It was afternoon, such a long afternoon, such a hot afternoon. The window was open and she sat by it letting the dust-laden draught touch her face and hair.

Hugh and Lili were in the room with her. The girl was saying, 'Do you think she would do anything silly?'

'I'd prefer it,' Hugh said, 'if you didn't lean out of the window like that, Carla.'

'I can't get away through the window.'

The girl said, in German, 'I don't trust her, Hugh.' They did that a lot, he noticed, switched from German to English, then back to German. Which was amusing since she understood everything they said.

'She's getting hysterical,' Lili said. 'You should slap her face.'

Hugh said in German, 'I'd rather not.' Then in English, 'Stop it, Carla. Snap out of it.' When she cowered under the window in case he tried to hit her, he said, 'I didn't realise she was as bad as this. Unless our devious Carla's playing Ophelia. Are you, by any chance, Carla?'

She refused to answer, making the two of them whisper together out of hearing. It was the girl who came over to touch her shoulder with a show of concern. 'Where are you, Carla?' the girl said.

'In my room.' She laughed, then said it in German: 'In meinem Schlafzimmer.'

'Do you know who I am?'

'Lili Marlene.'

'You try,' Lili said to Hugh.

'I've got this uncomfortable feeling the little shrew's pulling our collective leg. Who am I, Carla?'

'Carla's father.' After the slightest pause she added, 'Maybe.'

'Why don't you let me close that window?' To Lili he said: 'I'm damn sure she's taking us for a ride.'

'I don't want to go for a ride with you. I don't trust you enough. Girls should never go for rides with strange fathers,' she said. 'A man told me.'

'I think,' Lili whispered, 'you should telephone the doctor again.'

'It isn't worth it now,' he said, consulting his watch. 'What I'll do is let them know what to expect. The people at the other end. I'd better go and see to that now, I think. Meanwhile, I'd appreciate it if you'd stay with her. It's either that or nail the window shut.'

'Of course,' the girl said.

Why did they think it would help to nail up the window? What did the window have to do with it? It was the wardrobe they ought to be nailing up, the entrance to the cold room. What a pity she was so afraid to go back in there. The cold room really was the place where they blotted her out, after all. Those clouds. Those heavy, freezing clouds that iced up her mind and made it numb and motionless. She really was much safer here in her bedroom, where the clouds were thinner and their shadow merely cooled and slightly thickened her thinking. Here her thoughts only crept like cold oil around her brain. Once her brain thawed the thoughts would flow freely again and she would be all right. She knew that for certain. But for the time being the gaps were enough, those blue patches that would occasionally appear and disappear as the cloud thinned to mist, swirling over and back. With perfect timing the blue patches could be reached at a clear moment, plunged into . . .

Hugh was outside, under her window. He was getting into the car.

'Why's he gone out to phone?'

'Yes, he's gone to telephone.'

'Why's he gone out to do it? Why not use the one downstairs?'

'Bitte?'

'I didn't expect you to tell me.'

'There is no telephone in the hotel,' the girl said.

It happened so quickly that her own speed and strength took her by surprise. She heard the car start up, saw it drive away, and was shouting to Lili—'What's he doing? What's he doing?'—and pulling her urgently to the open window. And when the girl had stuck her head out to look she found she had all the time she needed to slam the heavy sash window down on her neck.

She would have liked time, too, to check if the neck was broken, but that hadn't been her intention. All she wanted was to get to the wardrobe.

'How many men in it?' Karl's question startled her. She must have dozed off.

'Couldn't tell. Think they want to tempt us out?'

'Why not just come in and get us?'

Christa shrugged. 'Maybe they think you've got a gun.'

'Smart girl.' He gave a bitter laugh. 'Was that a guess or did you know?'

'You have got a gun.'

'It's the only thing I didn't tell you. I was afraid you'd take it while I was asleep and use it on your father.'

'Oh, no,' Christa said, picking up the knife. 'This is for him.'

Karl shook his head. 'No, I've been thinking it out, Christa. I want you to go back. No, listen. There's a chance they may still not know about me. Whatever we think, we have to work on the assumption that they don't know. Now if that's so, nothing would be more suspicious than if you stayed missing. Just hear it through. Last night you had a scare. Natural enough. Questioned by the Gestapo, threatened by your father, etcetera. A girl would get scared. Anyone would. So what did you do? The most natural thing in the world. You panicked. You went up to your room, packed a bag and ran for it. You spent the night on a bench in the Tiergarten, say. Somewhere like that. Right, morning comes and you're cold and you realise how silly you were. So once again you do the natural thing and come home. "Forgive me, Vati, I acted like a child" and so forth.'

'Wouldn't work.'

'At least it would confuse them. If they're waiting for a move from us let's give them an unpredictable one. They'll want time to try and work out where you really went. It'll give us time, Christa.'

'What am I supposed to do? Just breeze into the shop half-way through the day and calmly put on my apron?'

'Why not? Frankly, you look as if you spent the night on a park bench.'

'Thanks. You know how to make a girl feel glamorous, you do.'

'Christina Söderbaum with red eyes, that's you.'

'I love you too.'

'I do love you, Christa.' He added lightly, 'From snout to trotter.'

'And you'd make a fair loin chop,' she told him.

'Butcher.'

'Pork lover.'

'My mother'd have a fit.'

Seeing him sadden, Christa said, 'She's probably complaining about the food for all she's worth right this minute.'

'She had a cold. When they took her away she had this cold. She's a terrible hypochondriac, my mother. But it was a genuine cold— Leni said she was in bed with it. They took her out of a warm bed, Christa.'

'They've done worse things.'

'Not to my mother. Christa, I want you to go back now. Dole out their matchboxes of meat, complain about the air-raids with the rest of them, predict Final Victory by winter, do whatever you normally do. And come back to me tonight.'

'Karl—'

'Don't forget to chat up Frau Holzbaum as well. I want you to be honeyed ham to everyone today. Even to your father. No, especially to your father.'

'If I knew,' Christa said, 'if I knew it would end in the worst way it could I'd do it all again . . . and again.'

'Don't worry,' he said lightly, 'they haven't got a rope in the Third Reich that would hold your weight.'

She poked out her tongue at him. He pulled her close. And while they were holding each other tightly he said, 'Save me a steak for

165

dinner,' and she answered, 'You can have Goering's special order,' knowing it was the last thing she would ever say to him.

'She's a maniac,' Lili was saying. 'She could have killed me.' She was sitting on the bed, clasping a cold compress to the back of her neck, her face white with shock and pain. Hugh was patting the girl's arm, as if that was where the hurt was. 'She's mad, Hugh. She really is not sane.'

Mad.

How pleasing it was to know, finally, the cause of everything.

Insanity. Wasn't one person in ten insane? It was nothing so abnormal, then, no horror in it, then. A little white-coated homunculus perched among the grey folds of her brain made the diagnosis, another voice, not herself at all, explaining it to her in the gentle, patient tones reserved for children, or imbeciles, or madmen; pronounced her curable. All she had to do was acknowledge one or two things.

That there was no Karl and never had been.

No space behind the wardrobe, no tapping.

That there was no plot and never had been.

No Moltke, no Schreiber, no Kreismann. No phone call.

No Christa.

That these were figures in a nightmare landscape in Carla Martin's mind, figures real and unreal mixed, ingredients of the waking dream who came and went at her will. Yes, like a brilliant dream. A fiction, an ingenious story so elastic in its plot that every sound, every impression could be placed within it, accommodated.

Like the car starting. Like the tapping. Like the half-heard voices in another room. All accounted for and placed by the inventive, infinitely flexible dreaming mind.

Except that she hadn't been dreaming.

Which was how she knew she was mad.

'I'm so sorry,' she heard herself say.

'You did it on purpose.'

'I'm not responsible.' Mad people were not responsible. It was a well known fact.

'If you don't go soon,' the girl said, rubbing her neck, 'she will miss her flight. I would not like that to happen.'

'Yes,' Hugh said, 'I think we'll make a move now. Don't want to leave it too late.' As he stood up she felt herself turn towards the wardrobe. It was a good feeling, looking at the wardrobe, knowing there was no Karl behind the wall to abandon or betray. How could he starve or be taken by the police if he didn't exist? She smiled, content now to be leaving, suddenly very happy because Karl was safe and could never die. 'Carla, it's empty,' Hugh said. 'It's been checked a dozen times. We've both checked it. Believe me, you've left nothing behind.'

Hugh went in front of her down the stone steps, the steps she'd crept down perhaps a dozen times to sneak food from the kitchen for her imaginary fugitive lover; the steps she'd stood on to eavesdrop on the fancied telephone conversation. In the corner formed by the staircase and the wall there was no telephone. It was almost a relief not to see one. With a detachment that surprised her she marvelled at the power of her own imagination. The school reports were right, the ones that always referred to her as 'a highly imaginative girl'.

And there, for the last time, was Frau Holzbaum, lurking, as always, in the hallway; dressed, as always, in brown. She looked—what? Relieved. Yes, Carla thought, that makes two of us, Frau Holzbaum.

'I hope she's better soon,' the woman was saying to Hugh. She was no longer a person, then, if everybody had to talk about her in the third person. People did that sometimes to older children who could quite well answer for themselves. 'How old is she?' they'd say to the parent. As a child she'd always answer, 'She's seven and she can speak for herself.' But now she merely ignored Frau Holzbaum, because the old bitch couldn't touch her any longer, and walked past her and into the street.

Here it was cool, cooler than in her room. The air smelled of rubble and sewers. She gulped at it as if breathing was a new exercise she hadn't quite got the hang of yet.

And there was the red car, perhaps a dozen paces away, facing right. Hugh went ahead of her to open the driver's door, which was on the opposite side from the pavement. In a moment he would open the passenger door and she'd be inside the car being driven away to a safe place to be made well again.

His movements were very slow and deliberate, as if he was waiting for something to interrupt him. An actor drawling his lines because the cue was late. That was odd. She'd expected him to be in a hurry to get her away. Wasn't he afraid she'd run from him at the last moment? Couldn't he see how urgent it was that she should get into the car *now*? The car was parked directly in front of the shop, after all. It could be seen, she could be seen from the shop window, and she could see *him* in there looking in her direction.

Now he was standing in the doorway of the shop in his apron yellow with fish guts, and—oh, God he was coming out while the man on the other side of the red car was fumbling with his keys to open the driver's door, the car's bulk between them so he couldn't see, couldn't see the big ox lumbering towards her across the pavement, calling her, grabbing at her with his stinking guts-reeking fat hands, couldn't hear the scream because her mouth wasn't functioning properly and the scream was a silent scream that never left her brain, couldn't help her, the man with the key, the stone man frozen for ever in his simple little act of opening the door of a small red car.

'And where do you think you're going?'

'Leave me alone, I'm going in aren't I?'

'Where've you been, slut?' She was busy tying on her apron and didn't answer him quickly enough. He moved to slam the side of his hand against her face, but just then a customer came in, a young, attractive woman Christa had seen in the shop before.

'Anything nice for me, Herr Bruckner?'

'Not if you call me that, my lovely.' He wagged his fat finger at her, reaching under the counter. The customer laughed.

'Rudi,' she said coyly.

'Little bit of belly.' He handed her a bloody paper parcel and patted his own beer belly at the same time. 'This isn't rationed, though.'

'My husband's leave's up on Tuesday.'

'Call round Wednesday. Might have a bit of belly for you.' He winked.

'Heard the latest?' the young woman said, leaning confidentially across the counter. Bruckner leaned too, so that his face came within kissing distance. The customer smiled and drew back fractionally. 'They say he's all right. Left before the bomb went off.'

'What's news about that? I could have told you that. Take more than a bastard bomb to kill the Führer, Ilse my lovely.'

'They've got all the stations cordoned off down town, machine guns and everything. Ernst might get recalled.'

'Wouldn't that be a shame?' When the customer had gone he said to Christa, 'Try and move that fish.' They were selling more fish these days. There was too little meat even for the ration demand. 'And I still want to know where you got to last night.'

'Tiergarten,' she said, gutting a fish with a single practised stroke.

'Whores' playground.'

'Suits me, then, doesn't it?'

'Don't bleeding well lip me, girl or you'll get this.' He showed her his fist. Fish scales clung to it. 'Anyway, no gallivanting around this afternoon, slut. Plots or no bloody plots, we're picking up an order in town. Understand?'

'Where?' That was puzzling. They weren't due to pick up an order, and he'd said 'town', so they couldn't be going to the slaughterhouse (thank God). And why go traipsing into town on a day when someone had tried to knock off Hitler?

'Never you mind where. Other side of town. You'll cut your fucking hand off in a minute.'

Shortly after four o'clock they were driving along Charlottenburger Chaussee. He'd tied her door shut so that she couldn't, as he put it, 'try any monkey business again', but she had the window open and was enjoying the rush of wind on her face. The Victory Goddess was painted black at Grosser Stern, so that she wouldn't be a landmark for the enemy bombers. But there were fewer raids now. Now it was a question of waiting to be shelled by the Red Army, which came nearer Berlin every day. Another four or five months, Christa was thinking, should see the war out. It would be hard living in the capital while the final allied offensive was mounted, but after that, if they survived the bombs and the shells . . . She wondered fleetingly how

Karl's mother would regard her as a daughter-in-law, a pork butcher's daughter, a Party member's daughter. Perhaps the year and a half she'd spent feeding and hiding the woman's precious son might make some difference to her attitude, but she doubted it. Anyway, the chances of Frau Silbermann surviving the camp . . . That made her feel guilty, as if she were responsible just because Frau Silbermann's 'removal' (how easily the euphemism came) would be convenient. Yet, for Karl's sake, let alone anything else, she wanted the woman to be alive, wanted her at the wedding. She would imagine a fat Jewish lady with rings on her fingers saying, 'What, my Karl couldn't do better for himself?'

Then, of course, there was the baby. How would she take *that*? No, she wouldn't think yet about the baby. Her period was only over-due a couple of days. She'd put off thinking about the baby (if there was a baby) for a bit.

Where were they now? The van had turned off somewhere. She glimpsed an army truck broadside across the road, and a group of soldiers manning a machine gun by it. Were they rebels or Govern-ment troops? That was a possibility worth considering, a coup against Hitler. If some of the more moderate elements could take over and make peace, say, with Britain and America, Karl would be safe and it would mean she wouldn't have the Ivans raping her. Not that it mattered which pig stuck his pizzle into you. There were worse things than being raped.

She thought they must be somewhere in the Zoo district. The van was stopping outside a bar Christa half recognised.

'I fancy a beer,' her father said. 'Want a drink?'

He lingered over the beer, which wasn't like him. The first one usually disappeared like rain down a gutter. He finished the half litre, then bought another. He seemed to be in no hurry to pick up his order. But when she asked him about the orders he laughed. 'Bollocks to the orders. We can pick up orders any time. Have something to wet your whistle, girl.'

And a thought started sliding about in her head. A thought like a bone in greasy hands, one that wouldn't stay still long enough to be grasped and looked at. It had to do with Karl, with Moltke, with her father suddenly so slow and content over his second beer in an hour. He was sitting there sunning himself, spreading his fat belly in the sun and waiting for time to pass.

She was on her feet, then, screaming at him. 'Take me back.' People passing stopped to see what the fuss was about. 'Take me back now,' she screamed. 'I want to go back.'

'Shut your trap,' he said. 'Have a bit of respect.' He laughed suddenly, enjoying the humour of his thoughts. Then he looked at his watch and said, 'You're too late, anyway, kiddo. Your bit of Kosher meat's not in the cold room any more.'

He shook his head, pulled at his beer, and laughed uproariously as if at the memory of a joke to end all jokes.

She spent the return journey staring mindlessly through the rear window of the van, sickened by what she now knew awaited her. They followed the same route back, along Charlottenburger Chaussee and through the Brandenburger Tor, where they were stopped and spot-checked by an army patrol. Wilhelmstrasse, she saw, was crawling with SS men. She wondered numbly how they found time to round up Jews on such a day, but that was Gestapo efficiency for you.

She'd expected the street to be quiet, the arrest already stale news and Karl long gone. Instead she found the scene of a recent gun battle. The glass of her bedroom window had been broken by a stray bullet and there were bullet holes around it and around the store room window. Most of its boards were holed and splintered. The street, too, showed evidence of the firefight—broken glass and blood spotting the paving. Christa was reminded of Kristallnacht, when the Jewish shops had been looted and the synagogues burned. She rubbed some of the blood with her shoe, hoping it was pure and Aryan, not Karl's, hoping the blood on the street meant he'd taken one of them with him. But it didn't really matter because Karl's blood would be in the cold room if it wasn't here, and he would be dead. An image of him hanging like a side of beef forced itself into her mind and refused to fade. Meat. And the butcher beside her was smiling, perhaps at the same thought.

A few groups of people still lingered even now, after it was all over, remnants of the much larger crowd there must have been during the battle. And there, of course, was Frau Holzbaum, Gretchen the blood-hound, pointing up at the window space as she gave her shot by shot account to some interested passer-by. As Christa moved closer she could hear Frau Holzbaum saying, 'There she is, that's the girl . . . her father's shop . . . used to be his meat store-room in the old days,' but what Frau Holzbaum had to say didn't interest Christa. Funny, she was thinking, that this had all been so predictable and yet so inevitable. As if nothing more than a slight memory lapse had been responsible for Karl's death. And she felt no more guilty than she would about having overlooked an order for liver sausage. Briefly it registered also, though in the same unimpressive way, that if Frau Holzbaum knew about her connection with Karl and that she had been feeding him for eighteen months, then Moltke must know too. Ah, well, if Moltke was waiting in her room to arrest her, it wouldn't do to keep him waiting.

She went up. Nobody tried to stop her or follow her.

Her room was in less of a mess than she had anticipated, as though somebody had taken care not to inconvenience her too much. The wardrobe had been pulled away from the wall, of course, and the thin board partition with which she had replaced the original door to make access easier—that had been ripped away. It now leaned against the wall, and was riddled with bullet holes. She smiled. Nobody had taken any chances on Karl being still alive. They'd probably entered via the shop as well, catching him in the classical pincer movement. The entrance to the cold room was now open like a bloodless wound. Out of it, like a maggot, came Moltke, smiling.

'I saw you from the window,' he said. 'Through one of the holes. Quite lucky you weren't here this afternoon or you might have been hurt.' He indicated the broken glass under the window of her room. 'He had a gun, you see, your "U-Boat". I'm sorry about the mess. One of my men was shot, but we got the Jew.'

She asked, 'Is he dead?'

'No, I'm told he'll recover,' Moltke said. 'You look relieved.'

'I'm not ashamed of it.'

'Why should you be?' Crossing to the window he picked out a

shard of glass from the frame and seemed to study it before he let it drop to the floor. 'Dangerous. Yes, he put up a good fight, your Jew. You don't mind, I hope, my referring to him as "your Jew". No offence intended, gnädiges Fräulein.' Without turning from the window, he said, 'It's a great pity he couldn't be taken alive.'

'I don't understand, Herr Moltke.' Christa made an effort to keep her voice even.

'His resistance made it impossible.' He sighed and shook his head. 'I would like to have known how long he was in there, for instance, and how he was fed. There were signs of a long occupation.'

'Eighteen months. Why did you say he'd recover?'

Moltke turned. 'I didn't, Fräulein Bruckner. I was referring to Lederer. My man. So he told you he'd been there eighteen months. I wonder what made him think he could trust you—perhaps because he mistook your humanitarianism when you gave him the broth for something else.' He suddenly clicked his heels and became official. 'I will see to it that you receive a commendation for informing us about the Jew, though you'll understand that publicity about these things . . .' He smiled at Christa. 'But the word gets around if placed in the right ears. That caretaker's wife, the Holzbaum woman—I understand she has an echoing ear.'

'Someone's been lying to you, Herr Moltke,' Christa said. 'I didn't denounce him.'

Moltke gave her a rebuking look. 'Your false modesty surprises me, my dear miss. To render information of this kind is to perform a valuable service to the State. I think that's how the phrase should go.' She began to speak, but he cut her off by producing a folded sheet of paper from his pocket. 'I have your letter here,' he said, unfolding it.

There were too many words to take in at a glance. When Christa tried to read the letter from the beginning she found that her mind and eye refused to stay on the lines. It was as if in a bored moment she'd picked up some abstruse scientific report or a coded message that she had neither the knowledge nor the patience to cope with. Only single words, isolated phrases registered, and her own unmistakable slanting hand.

. . . tapping . . . rats behind my bedroom wall . . . scraping sounds
. . . old meat store-room . . . filthy clothes . . . fed him some
broth . . .

Her eyes moved to the last line of the letter, immediately above
'Heil Hitler!' and her signature. The author had written: 'I assume
he is a Jew in hiding and wish to inform you of same.'

'It is to your father's credit,' Moltke was saying, 'as an Old Fighter
and personal acquaintance of Reichsmarschall Goering that he has
such a loyal and dutiful daughter. Good day, my dear Miss Bruckner.'

'Who wrote that letter?' she demanded. 'I didn't write it. And you
didn't. Not you, licking your stub of pencil when you write orders.
Not you.'

'What letter?' Bruckner said, smirking. 'Oh, that letter. You wrote
that, Christa. You write a nice letter, you do. Neat.'

And Frau Holzbaum baked her a cake, using a month's ration of
eggs, butter and sugar.

'I'm surprised you didn't hear him sooner, dear,' she told Christa,
'what with him being right behind your wall and everything.
Couldn't have been there long, could he?'

TWELVE

She thought she must have been wandering for hours because her feet were aching and the sun was very low when Hugh found her. It was an effort to recall who he was as he drove her through the streets in the small red car and talked about medical check-ups and flights, as if nothing was wrong but the state of her nerves and an untidy flight schedule. There was another flight in the morning, he was telling her. He seemed to think that important. And when she heard him say, 'I'll be sleeping in your room with you tonight,' she shrugged, because that really didn't matter at all.

Nor did it matter that he deliberately parked outside the shop again. The shop had closed for the last time. There was nothing left to sell. She felt Hugh's firm grip on her arm as he nudged her out through the passenger door and then followed that way himself, sliding across her seat, still keeping hold of her arm. She didn't blame him for that. Why should he trust her?

'Where's he gone?' she said.

'Where's who gone, Carla?'

'Rudi Bruckner. My father, the butcher.' She pointed at the derelict shop, then at the weathered signboard. 'R. Bruckner: Fleischer,' she read aloud, annoyed that Hugh was being so obtuse. But all Hugh would say was, 'No idea. Maybe Frau Holzbaum will know. She's lived here for donkey's years.' She didn't press. What did it matter if she lost track of the days or the hours? Karl was dead now, so nothing mattered any more. Nothing at all.

They were sealing her in.

Entombing her alive.

The window in the cold room had been bricked up. She tried to remember when that had been done. Late autumn, she thought, after the shop had closed. The war was lost and everybody knew it even though nobody said it, and inside her the baby was growing. It would be born, she'd calculated, on 2 April, 1945. She'd worked it out as accurately as she could.

After the shop had closed she'd got a job in an armaments factory. Her father, with no meat or fish left to sell, had gone into the Volkssturm. She worked a few weeks in the factory, filling shell casings with explosive, and nobody knew she was pregnant because her well-rounded figure could be due to the starchy foods they now had to eat on account of the shortages. Besides, she carried small. Then, in November it must have been, she'd begun to 'show' and one morning the factory boss sent her home as unfit. They needed children more than shells, he'd said. For the Fatherland.

And that was the day she'd moved her bedding into the cold room, in case Karl came back. She wouldn't want to miss him if he came back. She would sometimes pretend he was in there with her, and would lift her skirts to show him her swelling abdomen, let him pat it, let him press his ear to it and listen to the baby inside. Karl would lie on her mattress beside her and they would make love and talk in whispers. Once she'd showed him the knife and told him she was waiting till after the child was born to stick her father. Karl hadn't protested.

One night her father came home and found her in the cold room on her mattress. He'd had the Ilse woman with him, and the Ilse slut had said, 'She's nuts, Rudi.' So the Ilse woman, the slut whose husband had been killed in August, was going to be stuck too when the time came. 'I'll tell you something else,' the slut said, 'she's pregnant.' Her father had stared at her belly, then, beginning to understand. 'I'm a sausage,' she remembered saying to him, because her skirt fitted like a sausage skin.

'You've got yourself knocked up,' he'd told her, which made her laugh.

'You got me knocked up,' she said. That had got him. She'd never seen him move as fast before as he did to get his slut out of hearing. When he came back he said, 'I was pissed, wasn't I?'

'When aren't you pissed?'

'Watch that lip. I can still fatten that lip of yours.' Then, 'Well I'll be buggered. I never thought.' He'd laughed, plucked at a nostril thoughtfully with thumb and index finger. 'So bleeding what? It's good Aryan blood, ain't it? And good blood's good blood, right?'

'Even when it's half something else,' she'd said with a giggle.

His face had gone dark. He'd taken a step towards her with both fists clenched. 'What's that supposed to mean?'

'Even when it's half alcohol?' And she had laughed till the tight waistband of her skirt almost cut her in half.

That had been when he'd picked her up, rolled up in the mattress like a Frankfurter, and had carried her back into the bedroom.

Then he'd bricked up the cold room window, tearing away the splintered, bullet-riddled boards.

Then he'd nailed boards across the entrance to the cold room and screwed the wardrobe in place with four heavy screws, using all his strength to tighten them.

And now he was screwing planks over the window of her bedroom to seal her in. She watched him expressionlessly, stifling giggles. The slut was helping him, helping him carry his mattress into the room, where it was placed under the window.

'Would you rather I slept with her?' the girl was saying.

'No, she might be a bit much for you to handle. The doctor's coming soon to give her a sedative, but I'd better sleep here to be on the safe side.'

She slept.

She woke.

She slept again.

The dark was a suffocating blanket she tore at, a soft, smothering cloud that filled the room. She knew. Only the terrible covering darkness kept her from getting away.

She had to get away. She knew.

She had to get to Frau Holzbaum. Frau Holzbaum knew too, was the only one who did apart from herself. And Christa. Christa knew.

About the horror that was coming. What the horror would be, Christa knew that, but she, Carla, she only knew it was coming. Soon.

Gasping for breath, Carla groped her way to the window, but

177

there was no glass, only rough wood where the glass ought to be, which explained the darkness, the obliterating darkness.

It was vital not to panic. The room was dark because there were boards across the window. The window was in her bedroom, in a hotel, in a hotel in East Berlin, in 1972, and her name was Carla Martin, and she was almost sixteen, born in August 1956, and her best friend's name was Marsha and her father's name was Rudi . . .

No, Hugh. Hugh. Her father's name was Hugh Martin. And she was Carla Martin. And God she had to get out of this place.

She was beating on the boarded window with her fists and she was screaming. They would think she was mad, but it didn't matter what they thought. All that mattered was getting away. Now.

She heard a key turn in a lock behind her and the room became dazzlingly bright. She had to close her eyes to avoid being blinded. When she opened them again she saw the figure of a man approaching through a screen of water.

She began to whimper, then felt his touch on her shoulders, a gentle touch, and heard a gentle voice she knew saying, 'It's all right, Carla. It's all right. I'm here now.'

Her body shook as she sobbed into his shoulder. 'Hugh,' she said. 'You're Hugh.'

'Shh. There. It's okay. I'm here now.'

'Hugh . . .'

'Yes, darling, shh.'

There were no words to tell him. It was in her head, all of it, but she had no words to lever it out. 'You don't understand it,' she heard herself say.

He said, 'The doctor will be here soon. He'll give you something to make you sleep.'

'No. I've got to get away. Christa.'

'In the morning,' he said, soothingly, to a baby crying in the night.

'Now, now. You don't know. Frau Holzbaum. Where's Frau Holzbaum?'

'I won't leave you again,' Hugh said and stroked her hair. 'You were sleeping.'

And behind him the door was open.

Carla caught him off balance with a sudden hard push, so that he seemed to run backwards for a few short steps before he fell, a look of total surprise on his face as if running backwards was a feat he'd never managed to achieve before. Then she was out in the hall, pulling the door closed behind her.

The key was still in the lock and she turned it.

There were sounds coming from the kitchen.

If it was the kitchen.

If it wasn't the shop. She was afraid to go in to see who was making the sounds, though her need to find Frau Holzbaum before Hugh broke open the bedroom door was desperate. It wouldn't hold for long. But all she needed was a minute or two to get the answers from Frau Holzbaum. You see, she told herself, I have to know about your life, Christa, your terrible pitiable life which isn't my own life but which you let me share. But I don't want to share it all because I have a life of my own, dear Christa, my poor darling, and we're both so young. And I'm sure you understand, darling, that there must come a point where I'll have to leave you, and only Frau Holzbaum, bitch as we know she is, can tell Carla where that point is. Don't you see?

Christa was being difficult.

Christa was holding her back. And upstairs Hugh would be breaking down the door.

'Let go, damn you,' she said to the other girl. 'Let go.'

It hurt her to do it but she had to push the other girl roughly aside so that she could get into the kitchen.

'And don't follow me in,' she said as she entered.

Frau Holzbaum was in the kitchen. Christa had stayed outside after all, then, or this would have been the shop.

Or had she sneaked in? Because there was something probing inside her head that had no place there, and the something was scrambling her speech so that Frau Holzbaum wouldn't understand her.

Frau Holzbaum paled at the sight of her. She must look like a wild thing. She felt heavy and awkward as she waddled towards Frau Holzbaum, who dodged easily aside. Christa was doing it. Get away, can't you leave me alone for a minute?

179

'Christa,' she said to Frau Holzbaum.

'Don't come near me,' the old woman said. Ah, yes, she was old.

How that woman had aged. God, what a crone she'd become. Letting herself go like that because her old man had died.

'Christa wants to know if you wrote that letter. You see, she knows you denounced people all the time, and she wants to know if you gave Karl away.'

'I don't know anything,' Frau Holzbaum was yelling. 'Leave me alone.'

The old woman was moving in a wide arc towards the door. Carla could have cut her off, but Christa was too heavy, too sluggish. Why was Frau Holzbaum afraid, anyway? Hurting her wouldn't bring Karl back. 'Please help me,' she pleaded. 'You're the only one who knows. I only want to know.'

'I don't know anything. Who told you lies about me?'

It was then that Carla remembered the question she had come down to ask Frau Holzbaum, the question she'd gone to all that trouble to ask. But Hugh spoiled it. When he burst into the kitchen, wild-eyed, Carla felt her lip begin to tremble because he'd spoiled it for her, and now she'd never know.

'Thank God,' Hugh said, which made no sense at all.

And Frau Holzbaum said to him, 'I'm a trustee. I do my job, that's all. My record's clear, and this one's got no business stirring up trouble for me with her lies. Ask anyone about me. I never denounced anybody, Herr Martin.'

The question was still there in her mind. She tugged at it, but now Christa was sitting on it, and she couldn't budge it from under so much weight, though she wept with the effort.

The doctor was there, leaning over her. The same pinched-faced one again. She opened her legs. When you gave birth you had to open your legs even to this man's cold, dry fingers.

You had to push, too, to help the delivery.

So she pushed.

Her father was present at the birth, holding her down, and the slut

180

was holding her legs. The pain was like cramp, no, like terrible constipation.

She struggled against the pain, writhed on the bed, bearing down as she knew she must.

Then the doctor jabbed a needle in her arm. She heard him say, 'It won't put her to sleep, but she won't be doing much jumping around either.'

That was good. She wanted to see the baby's face as soon as it emerged, to see whose face it was. It would be Karl's, though. She was sure of that.

The building shook violently, almost throwing her off the bed. But by now she had the baby in her arms, so it hardly mattered that the world was coming to an end. She looked closely at the infant's face as she nursed it, and smiled when she saw the soft, blotchy face of a baby boy who looked exactly like Karl.

She held it up as the room shook again, held it up so that it could witness the end of the world: corpse-strewn streets and buildings in flame, and everywhere the sound of falling masonry, the whistle of rocket bombs. Outside, she knew, there were bodies dangling from the lampposts, signposted like thoroughfares: Traitor. Defeatist. The cardboard signs, crudely lettered, hung around their blackened necks like price tags.

Her baby, frightened by the noise of the world ending, cried most of the time.

Her father came and went, came and went. He was fighting somewhere in the northern suburbs with his Volkssturm unit, but each time he returned home, she noticed, he was still alive. It annoyed her.

On one of these visits she heard him remark that the tide would turn soon. They were pushing the Red Army back, he said, and the Führer, he told her, was saying the same thing, so it must be true.

Then he tickled the baby under the chin and said, 'You should have hung on in there a few more days, little Hermann, and then you could have been born on the Führer's birthday.'

She went out to fetch water from a well in the street because something had happened to the mains supply. Some of the tenants were leaving the building, too, which was puzzling. She asked Frau Holzbaum about it. Frau Holzbaum said, 'When the Ivans get here they'd better not find you here, I can tell you. Not with your father a Party man. I can tell you.'

Then, one day, while she was giving baby Karl his midday feed, Frau Holzbaum came in carrying a suitcase. 'You're the last one,' she said, which didn't make sense. 'We're going now. To my sister's place. You better get out while you can.' She thanked Frau Holzbaum for thinking of her and little Karl, and it saddened her to remember that she'd never liked the caretaker's wife, who wasn't a bad sort after all. 'Seen my baby?' she said, holding Karl up to be admired, but Frau Holzbaum had already gone.

She took baby Karl out for a walk. Somebody forgetful had left a pram in the middle of Prenzlauer Allee with bundles of dirty clothing in it. She threw out the washing and wheeled Karl along in the pram instead. Later, she thought, I'll put the pram back exactly where I found it.

They stopped to watch the pretty lights in the sky. Karl enjoyed watching the different coloured lights but was afraid of the noise, so she took him home again. On the way they had to stop because the road was blocked by a building that had fallen down. Someone was screaming in the ruins. She thought: 'What a silly place to sit and scream,' and told the baby so. It made him laugh.

And there were people, some in uniform, some with babies in prams or in their arms, running towards the city centre. She wondered where they were all going and why; felt left out because they were probably all going somewhere quiet and cosy and she hadn't been invited. She didn't care. Not as long as she had baby Karl.

Then her father came home again, still alive. She sighed. He looked so dirty that she didn't want to let him hold Karl. He snatched the child away from her, looking angry. 'What the fuck are you still doing here?' he said. 'It's finished.'

'We live here,' she told him. He was even more stupid than she'd imagined if he'd forgotten that.

'Stupid bitch. You've gone right off your rocker this time. The Ivans are streets away.'

'I'm not a Party member,' she said, remembering what Frau Holzbaum had told her. 'Neither is Karl,' she added.

'Karl? Who's bloody Karl?'

He really was stupid. She wondered if the bombs might have made him a little mad.

'You're Karl, aren't you, little darling?' she said to the baby, smiling at him, rocking him.

'Hermann,' Bruckner said. 'The kid's name's Hermann. Can't even remember your own bleeding kid's name, you crazy cunt.'

'Don't swear in front of Karl. And he's mine, so you can't say what his name is. He's all mine.'

'Me and Ilse are getting the hell out,' Bruckner told her. 'Me, I'm off. You can stay and open your legs for the whole fucking Russian army if you like, but I'm off. And I'm taking the kid with me.'

She covered the baby's head with her hand and clutched the child protectively. 'He's not yours to take,' she said. She bent over the baby's face and cooed into it. 'You're my Karl's ickle baby, aren't you? Yes, you are. Yes.'

A 'Stalin Organ' exploded close by, making the building shake.

'You better not be saying what I think you're saying,' her father said very quietly. So quietly that she could hardly hear him above the noise.

She found it funny. The war was teaching her such a lot about people.

First Frau Holzbaum, whom she'd never liked, had been nice.

Now her father, a hateful man, was being nice too. Perhaps wars did that to people, changed them from nasty to nice. If so, wars had a lot to be said for them.

It might be because the Russians were coming and didn't like members of the Party. He might want her to say nice things about him to the Ivans when they came, tell lies about what they'd done to big Karl in the cold room. But that seemed unfair. She didn't think she could do that.

Far off, she could hear her baby crying. Downstairs somewhere. He'd taken the baby for walkies.

Then why was little Karl crying downstairs? Not just crying.

Screaming with all the power of his tiny lungs, poor darling. He wanted his mummy.

She started down the stone stairs to find out why Karl was screaming like that, but the screaming stopped abruptly before she was halfway down. She went back upstairs to wait for the treat he'd promised her. She couldn't recall the last time he'd promised her a treat. And now that she thought about it, she was very hungry, which made her milk thin. There wasn't anything to eat in the house and the shops were all closed, but he was going to cook them all a lovely dinner. He'd said so.

They were eating in her bedroom, sitting at her dressing table. Why not off that big wooden table in the kitchen? And where was Ilse? It was just her father and herself. He was eating and she was lying on her bed.

'Ah, you're awake,' he said.

'Where's mine?' she said.

Then he started to carve the meat. It smelled delicious. She was literally faint with hunger, so that her legs wobbled as she got off the bed. The smell of the food was painful to breathe, like the air of an oven.

'Which half do you think you ought to have?' he was asking her, and she said, 'the breast,' because it was her favourite. What was it? A chicken? Where had he got a chicken from?

'I'm glad you're hungry,' her father was saying. 'It's a good sign.' She noticed now how much weight he'd lost. He'd gone quite thin, wasn't a big man any longer. But she'd never seen him looking so neat. Then his voice changed as he said, 'No, I mean the Kosher half or the other half? Light meat or dark?' And he seemed to find that very funny. He put the carver down on the dressing table and doubled over with laughter. When he got back enough control to be able to speak he said, 'What was that Jew king's name?' and she said, 'What?' and he said, 'The Jew king.'

She didn't understand that. Hunger affected the brain, they said, made you light-headed. Well, that was a true fact, that was.

She began to cram meat into her mouth and chewed until her jaws ached and swallowing became difficult. Her mouth was too dry. She was about to ask him to give her a glass of water when he told her what it was she was eating. Then he sat back in his chair and waited to see how she would react.

The smile was still on his face when she stuck him to the heart.

She began to carve him, just as he'd taught her.

The knife was blunt and wouldn't cut.

Funny, because last time it had carved him beautifully. She looked to see what was wrong. She laughed at her own silliness when she found out what was wrong. It wasn't a knife at all. It was a screwdriver.

The plastic handle and a few centimetres of the round steel blade were sticking out of his shirt. It looked comical, as if a screw had come loose in his heart and she'd been trying to fix it. Silly girl.

But the face troubled her. There was something wrong with it.

It wasn't smiling. It looked surprised. And afraid. And in death it looked somehow . . . different.

Her father's face, yet a stranger's face. Looking at it made her feel weak and faint, and as she stretched for the memory it was swamped by a rising wave of nausea.

She vomited until only colourless fluid trickled from her mouth.

Afterwards she felt clean and bright inside. Now all she had to do was hide. Somewhere she could never be found.

The lock on the bedroom door was broken, its tongue warped. It had been levered with a crowbar, perhaps that screwdriver. She hadn't done it, had she? No, the man on the floor, the dead one whose name she couldn't remember, he must have done it. What was his silly name? Heinie?

Hugh.

Her mind skipped.

His name was Hugh and he was a stranger. So why had she killed him?

The question nagged at her as she descended the stairs. It was more important at the moment to worry about nosy Frau Holzbaum catching her. But Frau Holzbaum had gone to stay with her sister, hadn't she? She must have, because she didn't poke her head out.

Now she was in the street. A red car was parked at the kerb outside the shop. But nobody was inside the car, and that was all that mattered. She mustn't be seen going into the shop. She hesitated.

It was all wrong. Where the shop door ought to have been was a small window with louvred vents in it which poured forth steam. Like a laundry or a kitchen. And where the shop front should be someone had nailed sheet metal cladding.

She looked up to the cold room window, but that was bricked in now. Of course. That she did remember. And there, to the right of it, were the boards her father had screwed over the broken glass of her window to stop her getting out. You could still see the bullet holes in the surrounding masonry.

The shop wasn't the way in, then. Not these days. When Rudi Bruckner closed a shop he really closed it. So it would have to be the other way, through the wall.

She went back upstairs as carefully as she could in case Frau Holzbaum heard her.

The man still lay on the floor waiting to have his heart-screws tightened, waiting very patiently. She felt like apologising when she pulled the screwdriver out of his chest, wrenching and turning it because it was stuck fast in the muscle. You had to have the technique to do that. She knew the technique because her father had taught it to her once, long ago, so long ago she couldn't remember when.

It was essential to be quick now. She had to get into the cold room before anyone came looking for thingummy—had to get where nobody would think of looking for her.

God, those bloody screws were tight. The bastard had used all his strength on them. But she was a pretty strong girl, even if she was undernourished these days. She had to wipe the screwdriver carefully first, though, to get all that slippery stuff off it. She wiped it on Heinie's shirt—he wouldn't mind, being dead. She giggled at that thought.

The work made her sweat like a pig. More weight off her frame. She'd soon be as thin as Carla, which was even more hilarious seeing as she was Carla. What a giggly mood to be in when there were these serious things to be done. She tried to assume a serious expression, but the effort made her laugh again and she had to sit down in the wardrobe to recover. Two out, two to go. She'd never get in there at this rate.

The third screw was a bastard. Every millimetre of its rusty thread fought against her, fought like a cat with its claws in a tree. But once her first sweat had cooled she found the work quite easy. She seemed to be getting more energy from somewhere, as if someone was helping her turn the screwdriver.

Then, finally, the last screw came free.

The heavy wardrobe squeaked as she pulled at it, caught on an edge of lino and took a sheet of the crumbly stuff away with it. But it was away. There was a space behind it big enough to crouch in—good thing she was so slim. Dumpy old Christa wouldn't have managed.

Only the planks left. These had to be prised away with the screwdriver (trusty old screwdriver) one by one. The wood was very dry and the nails made creaking sounds as they popped out, two at a time, two to a plank.

It stank.

The hole in the wall stank. There were sort of scurrying sounds coming from inside it, so she supposed it must have mice. Well, it had been sealed up a long time. Not surprising, really.

She wished she had a light so she could see what she was doing. The next job was one she'd need light for. Wait a sec, wasn't there a nightlight in the wardrobe? She went back and rummaged around on the wooden floor of the wardrobe and found a small lamp there. Its batteries were almost gone, though. When she pressed the switch a faint yellow glow came out. But it would have to do. The other thing she found there was a length of cord, the draw-string from a duffel bag. She took that with her, too, coiled up in her pocket.

Carrying the lamp between her teeth and with the dry old planks in her arms, she crawled on her knees and elbows into the cold room.

It was much darker than she remembered. Even the small amount of light leaking in from her bedroom couldn't touch the thick, years-old blackness of the cold room. It was as if the darkness had been accumulating in there over the years, gradually filling the place up. And when it had got full, and there was nowhere for the dark to go, it had started compressing itself, thickening up, packing itself in as densely as it could.

But she wasn't going to think about that now. There was more to do.

The next thing was to shift that monstrosity of a wardrobe back into position. She placed one of the planks against its back, horizontally, and used one of the four screws to fix the piece of wood to it. Then, with this bar as a grip for her left hand, and with her right hand curled around the wardrobe's side, she began to drag the thing, millimetre by slow millimetre, back, uncaring about the noise of it, back to the wall. And as the gap closed the thin wedge of light from her bedroom got thinner and thinner in a pleasing kind of way, like a waning moon, till the wardrobe was flush with the wall.

The darkness wrapped itself around her. She had to hold the lamp between her teeth and very close to the work to complete the operation. This involved screwing the other plank to the back of the wardrobe at one end, and to the wall of the cold room at the other.

Two planks, four screws. Two to a plank. One in the wardrobe, one in the wall. The neatness of it delighted her.

She was tiring quickly now. The screwdriver kept slipping out of the screw slots in the darkness, burring them badly. But she had enough strength left to make a good job of it. She'd always had stamina. With the last of her energy she gave each of the four distorted screw heads a final quarter turn, then a final eighth of a turn, until the screwdriver could get no further purchase and no more turning was possible.

Weak, she let the tool fall to the floor and took a deep breath.

Now the wardrobe would be immovable from the outside.

Nobody would know she was in there.

She was safe.

Hungry, but safe.

Something brushed against her leg. She jerked it away. It had been a furry thing, quite large. A rat, probably.

There were rats in here. In the swarming darkness. The lamp shone the colour of pale lemon and was dimming noticeably. When she directed its anaemic beam up towards the ceiling she could barely make out the steel gleam of the meathooks hanging there.

Soon the batteries would die. The darkness would blind her. And already the hunger was making her too weak to fight off the rats, which were getting bolder. Several times in the past few minutes she'd felt them brush against different parts of her body.

Was that someone screaming she could hear?

Not herself. Surely not herself. From beyond the wall, from her bedroom. That was where the screaming was coming from. And voices.

She couldn't hear what they were saying, not even with her ear to the back of the wardrobe, but there were definitely people talking in there.

A rat made a try for her throat and she found all she could do was brush it weakly away. Don't panic. Unscrew the screws.

She groped around for the screwdriver, not daring to wander too far from the back of the wardrobe. Thank God, she thought, when her nerveless fingers touched it. It took a great effort even to grip the handle. And when she tried to find a screw slot she found herself trembling too much to fit the blade into it. Besides, no strength left to turn screws.

How crazy it was not to have the energy left to scream, to have to turn all the panic and horror she was feeling inwards. Crazy, too, to hear your own voice talking in the tones of hysteria from a long way off, though really it must be inside your head you were hearing it.

And Frau Holzbaum's voice. But not inside her head. The voices were coming from the bedroom, from the other side of the wall. Her own voice and Frau Holzbaum's voice. All she had to do was call out to them, make them hear her. Hammer on the back of the wardrobe. They'd hear that. She'd have to be quick, before Carla and Frau Holzbaum went away. Carla would hear her, Carla would save her from the rats.

She hammered with all the strength in her body. Once, twice, three times. But she was so feeble now that her hammering was a gentle sound she could scarcely hear herself.

From the other side of the wall it would sound like tapping.

SHROPSHIRE COUNTY LIBRARY

DATE DUE	DATE DUE	DATE DUE	DATE DUE

PLEASE

return this book to the library from which it was borrowed on or before the date due; it may be renewed if not required elsewhere.

Look after the book; loss or damage must be paid for.

TO RENEW PLEASE QUOTE THE LAST DATE STAMPED AND DETAILS GIVEN IN PANEL ABOVE.

L.12